n Sixth
'' Road, Luton Beds.

Yo!
Diary! 2
And another thing . . .

*Once upon a time, Johnny (Jonathan to his biological parents) Meres
was a merchant seaman and an ice-cream man.
More recently, as a stand-up comedian, he has won the
Time Out Award For Comedy and been nominated for
The Perrier Award. He has written for and appeared on many radio
and TV programmes, including his own series for
BBC Radio 4. He lives in Edinburgh with his wife, two sons
and no cats. He was once fifteen.*

Yo! Diary! 2

And another thing . . .

Jonathan Meres

Piccadilly Press • London

To my current wife, Fiona,
for continuing to put up with me.

Oh, and thanks to Catriona and Peter H.

First published in Great Britain in 2000
by Piccadilly Press Ltd.,
5 Castle Road, London NW1 8PR

Text copyright © Jonathan Meres, 2000
Cover photographs © Katie Vandyck, 1999

Phototypeset from author's disc in 11/18.5 pt Chianti

A catalogue record for this book is available
from the British Library

ISBNs: 1 85340 661 9 (trade paperback)
1 85340 666 X (hardback)

1 3 5 7 9 10 8 6 4 2

Printed and bound by Creative Print and Design (Wales),
Ebbw Vale

Text and cover design by Judith Robertson

FEBRUARY

Seb • **FEBRUARY 15th**

Yeah, and another thing, man. Being an artistic visionary 24-7 can be both a blessing and a curse. Because like, you know, here I am, the chilled out morning after the seriously banging night before, when I should really be basking in the afterglow of what was, let's face it, an awesome night behind the decks, and already I'm thinking OK, been there done that, what now? Because you've got to keep moving, dude. You've got to keep pushing back those barriers. Like last night. There was some serious barrier pushing going down last night, man. The way I lulled them into a false sense of security with all that Bloke-U-Like and Westfield pap and then all of a sudden, BAM!! Straight in with a blast of my totally revolutionary Hardcore-Speed-Opera!! Yo! DJ Sebsonic was not only *in* The House. He *owned* The House, man!! You could tell by the way that everybody just, you know, stopped dancing and stared at me, admiration and total full-on respect written all across their faces. It was beautiful. I tell you, man, that Valentine's Disco will be talked about for a seriously long time to come. Years from now, hundreds of thousands of people will claim that they were there. The legend will grow and grow. No doubt, dude!

Clare • FEBRUARY 15th

Did something last night. I've got no idea what it was mind you, but I definitely did something. That's frightening, isn't it? I must be getting old! Well I mean, I *am* getting old. I'll be 17 in a couple of months!! My life seems to be flashing past in one big blur at the moment. Before I know it I'll be twenty! That's practically pensionable, isn't it? Why not just give me my bus pass right now and be done with it? God I'm depressed. What *was* it I did last night? There was music. And bright lights. Nope, it's gone again. I'd better finish now. If I hurry I might just make it down to Sofisticutz. Get one of those curly blue rinse perm jobs. Aye, just like all the other wrinklies.

Steven • **FEBRUARY 15th**

Disco last night. Went 2 C Clare. Looked gr8. Asked me 2 dance but music went rubbish so every1 left. Un4tun8ly.

Meera • **FEBRUARY 15th**

I suppose I should have known what I was letting myself in for, shouldn't I? I mean, I don't exactly need Psychic Sue or Kosmic Kate to tell me that Seb's never going to be a 'conventional' boyfriend, do I? Let's face it, the guy's a one-off. Well, in Molton Sodbury he is, anyway! Not that he is my boyfriend. Not officially anyway. Yet. OK, so if you want to get picky you could say that he's a friend. And he's a boy. So in that sense, yeah, I suppose you could say he's my boyfriend.

Ohmygodohmygodohmygod! What exactly am I trying to say here? We're seeing each other, that's all. Yeah, *seeing* each other. Not that Seb *saw* very much of me last night at the disco. I saw plenty of him though! Couldn't exactly miss him, mind you. Up there, grinning

7

and waving his arms about like he's Fatbloke Slim or someone! But I might as well not have been there at all for all the attention he paid me. But that's Seb for you, I guess. Take him or leave him, maaaan! And you know something? Call me crazy but I think I'll take him. For now, anyway!

Mandy • FEBRUARY 15th

Seb was bang out of order last night if you want my opinion. Or even if you don't! OK, so he had a job to do but he could have at least acknowledged that Meera existed! You know, a quick word, a smile, even an occasional bit of eye contact. But no, there he was, the big superstar DJ! Yeah right, in his dreams! What is it he calls himself again? DJ Sebsonic? Ha! DJ Substandard, more like! I think I'm going to have to have a word with him anyway. Mess with my best friend and you mess with me, mateypants!! Actually it's times like this makes me quite glad I'm not 'seeing anyone' at the moment as Meera so quaintly puts it. Seeing anyone my foot! Giving it the old tongue sandwich more like! Don't get me wrong. I'm not suddenly anti-bloke or anything stupid. Ha! Fat chance of that! Nothing I like better than a quick bout of Tonsil Gymnastics! No, it's just that right now, I'm quite happy that I'm not actually going out with anybody. I'm just happy playing the field basically. Woooof!!

Craig • FEBRUARY 15th

Went to the Valentine's Disco last night. Can't believe it's a year since the last one. But it is. Whoa, a whole year! Think about everything that's happened. Yeah, and one thing that still *hasn't* happened, if you get my drift. But it's a start, isn't it? Going out with Mandy, I mean. Who knows what might develop? Here's hoping anyway! For now though we're playing it cool. Yeah, *very* cool as it happens. So cool in fact that we hardly spoke to each other last night. Well we couldn't anyway. The racket Seb was making was just unbelievable. I did try and say something once. I had to get really close. Cupped my hand over her ear. Felt her hair in my face. I could almost smell her! It was fantastic! I said, 'How's it going?' She looked at me and shouted 'What?!!' That's one thing I really like about Mandy. Great sense of humour!

Seb • FEBRUARY 17th

Yo! Check this out, right? Mandy Miller has finally succumbed to the lure of The Sebmeister and wants my body big-time, basically! Not that I'm surprised or anything. They all do eventually. OK, so some take longer than others, but once a babe-magnet, always a babe-magnet! I should have warned her years ago. Resistance is futile, baby! Anyway she wants to see me tomorrow after school. She told me herself! Just came out with it! I tell you, man, that chick is one up-front dudess. But I'm just going to have to let her down gently. Tell her to join the back of the queue basically. Yeah, and remind her that I'm already going out with her best friend!

Mandy • FEBRUARY 18th

Honestly, what is Seb like? The arrogance of the guy is truly gobsmacking! Assuming that I wanted to go out with him! He's either incredibly stupid, or actually really rather sweet and naïve. I can't make my mind up which. He said he was really flattered but that he wasn't into two-timing Meera! At least I think that's what he said. You can never be too sure with Seb! I can't believe he actually thinks I'd do that to Meera though. All right,

10

so I snogged What's-his-face that time at the Christmas fair. But that was a one-off. OK, a two-off! But this is different. Meera's actually going out with Seb. Thinking about it though, Seb did pretty much tell me what I wanted to hear. I mean he obviously really likes her. So there's no problem basically. But I put him straight anyway. Told him I'd rather have toothpicks inserted under my fingernails one by one than go out with him. And I warned him that that's exactly what I'd do to him if I ever found out he was messing Meera about. I think he got the message.

Seb • **FEBRUARY 18th**

Mandy definitely fancies me.

Meera • **FEBRUARY 18th**

Seb just called me on my mobile. Told me he's really sorry we didn't talk the other night at the disco and what did I think of his 'kicking tunes' and 'banging beats'? I said that's OK, and that I thought his 'kicking tunes' and 'banging beats' were 'well hard, man'. I hope that was the right thing to say because to be honest I've no idea what it meant. Seb seemed happy enough anyway. I guess he'd be pretty hurt if he ever found out that I really think his 'beats' and 'tunes' are a big pile of steaming pants. But that's the beauty of a diary I suppose. He *won't* find out! OK, so I'm not being totally honest and I don't feel particularly good about that. But it's early days. I don't want to do anything that might jeopardise our relationship. No, I'll leave *that* to Mandy! (Just joking by the way, Mand! Love ya really, babes!) Anyway he's coming round again next week to do a bit more 'French revision'. Hmm, wonder what my parents would say if they found out Seb doesn't actually *do* French!

Clare • FEBRUARY 21st

Isn't there some saying about how you only realise how much you liked something when you can't get your hands on it any more? There must be. If there isn't, there should be! See I've been thinking. And wondering. Wondering about me and Seb and what might have been, blah blah blah. Wondering whether we might even have been good for each other? In a weird kind of way, obviously. Who knows, perhaps we still could be good for each other? Nah. It's history now. Time to file and exit, girl. Time to wake up and smell the decaff. It was only ever a brief attraction anyway. Aye, *very* brief, if I remember correctly. What on earth did I ever see in the guy? I mean, what about all that stuff he used to spout? All that Spokesdude For A Generation garbage! No it was definitely for the best that we never got it together. Future generations will thank us one day! I mean, think about it. What a genetic nightmare that would have been! Best of luck by the way, Meera. God knows you're gonna need it!

Steven • FEBRUARY 21st

Got 2 keep short 2day. 2 much 2 do. 2 much 2 clean. So little time. Mission 2 obliter8 all mess. Mess = misery = more mess. Fish fingers 4 T.

Mandy • FEBRUARY 22nd

Hmmm, 25 days in showbiz and not a single call from my agent. Actually I still can't get used to saying that. '*My* agent'! Sounds dead glam, doesn't it? Well he'd better call soon, that's all I can say. I'm going to look pretty stupid if he doesn't. Wish I hadn't told everyone now. But I was so excited I just had to! It's all I've ever wanted. Fame and fortune! What's wrong with that?

Absolutely nothing! Big posh house with a swimming pool? Yes please! Different colour car for each day of the week? Yeah, why not? Hello, is that the blonde one from Westfield? It is? In that case be round at my place in ten minutes! So what if I sound vacuous and shallow? Since when has daydreaming ever been a crime? Anyway I'm not saying I want to be filthy rich or anything. Hey, I'd settle for just being comfortably off! Just as long as Mum didn't have to work all hours to support us lot. It'd be nice to do a bit for her for a change, you know what I'm saying? Buy her a new dress or something. Take her to a nice restaurant . . . Yeah, *then* buy a big posh house and a flash car!! Ha ha!!

Craig • FEBRUARY 23rd

Me and Mandy are still playing it cool. I'm OK about it though. I mean, if that's the way she wants to play it then fine. Mind you, it would be quite nice if we actually spoke to each other once in a while. You know, more than just saying hi. But then when you've got a good thing going on with someone and when you feel really comfortable with that someone, then you don't necessarily *have* to talk. It's all in the body language. Apparently anyway. Yeah, well I was looking at this book of my sister's the other day, wasn't I? *Men Are From Margate, Women Are From Vauxhall* it's called. All about relationships and the differences between men and women and all that. It was a bit boring actually. Weren't even any pictures. Anyway I had to stop reading it because my sister came in and caught me! Yeah, just what I need. *Another* reason for her to take the mickey!

Seb • FEBRUARY 24th

Supposed to be going round to Meera's tomorrow night. Well, I mean I *am* going round to Meera's tomorrow night. It's just that, well, you know, I'm still not totally used to this whole boyfriend/girlfriend vibe yet. Don't get me wrong, man. I mean I'm well into Meera. That is most definitely for real! No doubt, dude! She's funny, she's seriously pretty and whilst she might not quite be my intellectual equal just yet, she's certainly no fluffy airhead either, you know what I'm saying? She can talk about stuff other than babies and pop stars, which is, you know, pretty unusual for a chick. No, it's just that it doesn't seem that long ago since I was dissing the whole idea of relationships. Wouldn't even think about it. Then, all of a sudden . . . well I'm in one basically! Dunno, man. I feel like I'm about to dip my toe into The Sea Of Conformity or something and, you know, test how cold the water is. I feel like I'm teetering on the precipice of Mt Conventional and finding out that I might just be afraid of heights! But hey, just because on the outside I *appear* to be turning into some kind of Joe Normal, doesn't mean to say that I actually *am*, dude! Yeah right. As if!

Meera • FEBRUARY 25th

Seb's just been round for another evening of 'French revision'. Yeah, in other words, talking and messing around! Not *that* kind of messing around, by the way! Fat chance of that with Mum and Dad watching 'Eastside Street' in the next room! Dad's probably got the place bugged and staked out with CCTV cameras anyway! Besides, Seb hasn't even tried to kiss me yet. I think he might have been just about to hold my hand at one point. But then Dad came in. It was a bit of a giveaway really because Seb leaped off the sofa like a rocket and went the colour of beetroot. Dad was amazingly cool about it though. Yeah, the trouble was, he started speaking French and asking Seb loads of questions! I swear I had no idea my dad could even speak French! Talk about a man of mystery! And guess what? Seb never batted an eyelid. He just smiled and nodded, like he could understand every word! Then he just started speaking back. In English! But with this really heavy French accent! I thought, Oh no, here we go. Fireworks time! But Dad just burst out laughing. I couldn't believe it. Then afterwards, when Seb had gone, Dad told me what a 'nice young man' he thought he was!! I'll repeat that. *My dad* thinks *my boyfriend* is a 'nice young man'! Will wonders never cease?! Is Mercury rising in Aquarius or something? I mean I know Psychic Sue has been warning to 'expect the unexpected' but this is ridiculous!

Craig • FEBRUARY 26th

Mandy, Mandy
Sweet as sugar candy
Lives just round the corner
Which is definitely handy.

Clare • FEBRUARY 27th

Parents, eh? You can't live with them and you can't live with them! Take mine for instance. Hey, I wish someone would! Honestly, they're like a pair of wee kids, they really are. At each other's throats all the time, like a couple of bickering polecats! They should just grow up. You know, act their age and not their shoe size! They were at it again tonight. Sniping and griping at each other. It wouldn't be so bad if it was over something really important. But it never is. It's always something completely petty and trivial, like whose turn it is to make the tea, or who's got custody of the TV remote! And the thing is, they're quite happy to do it in front of me. Perhaps they don't even realise they're doing it any more. Perhaps it's become second nature to them. Or perhaps they think I'm old enough and mature enough to be able to handle it now. Yeah, like that's supposed to make me feel better or something? Well surprise surprise, Mum and Dad! It *doesn't!*

Steven • FEBRUARY 28th

Favour8 day 2day. Double Biology = double Clare. But Clare not herself. Not on gr8 4m. 1der Y? Didn't dare ask. Does her room need tidying? 1der if I should of4?

MARCH

Mandy • **MARCH 1st**

Got an interview for a job at Safebury's tomorrow. Executive Financial Retail Operative to give it it's full title. Oh all right then, Checkout Assistant. Who cares? It's a job, isn't it? And we definitely need the money. I can't expect Mum to keep stumping up every time I want a CD or a new pair of shoes. She's finding it hard enough just paying the bills at the moment. Not that she ever moans about it, but I know she is. And it'll give me something to do while I'm waiting for that call from Hollywood! Oh god, what if they call while I'm at work? Sorry Mr Spielberg but Amanda's on a late shift today. Shall I get her to call you back? Aaaarrgghh! Nightmare! Anyway, first things first. The interview.

Hmm, what shall I wear? Now if *that*'s not a good excuse to call Meera, I don't know what is!

Craig • MARCH 2nd

Just sneaked another quick look at my sister's book. You should see the differences between men and women! There are loads! I thought it was all going to be stuff like . . . well, like the fact that men like football and women . . . don't basically. But it was all much deeper than that and dead intellectual. Well, the bits that I could understand were anyway. For instance, men are rubbish at communicating and women aren't. You know, women talk over any problems they've got and blokes just bottle them up and well, you know . . . Anyway it really made me think. Next time I'm worried about something I'm definitely going to talk about it. Not with my sisters obviously. And not with Dad either, because he's a bloke and even more rubbish at communicating than me! I could talk to Mum though. But what would I say? Mum, I think I might just be the oldest virgin in Northern Europe? Yeah right. I'd sooner City got relegated again. Oh, I don't know. Stupid book.

Meera • MARCH 3rd

Just called Mandy on the mobile and found out she got the Safebury's job! I knew she would. She just gives off this aura of confidence when she walks into a room. I guess it's the fire sign in her. Of course it might just have had something to do with the little black number I told her to wear at the interview! Well I figured she might as well wear something a bit glam while she still could. Let's face it, those stripy green nylon coats aren't exactly guaranteed totty-magnets, are they?! Hey, maybe that's my vocation in life! To work in fashion. Be a Personal Stylist to the stars, or something? Maybe even get to meet Leo De Janeiro!! Ohmygodohmygod you should see the centre spread of him in this month's *Almost 17*!! Not only that but you get a free sachet of this absolutely gorgeous sprout 'n' lavender body lotion. Sounds gross I know, but it's actually totally wicked!

Mandy • MARCH 4th

First day at work. Boooor-ring or what? I think the highlight of the whole day was probably changing the till roll (phew, so that extensive training last night obviously came in well handy, then), although watching my nail varnish dry did come a close second! As for the scintillating conversation with the rest of the girls? Well, there wasn't any basically. It was all what they were going to give their so-and-so for tea, or what their little what's-his-face had been up to at school. Half an hour of that and I was sticking staples in the back of my hand just for something to do! As for the uniform? I tell you, those nylon coats are better than any kind of contraception. Because, let's face it, no one's ever going to come anywhere near you when you're wearing one of those things! Oh well, think of the money, Mand. Let's face it, it's the only reason you're doing it!

Mandy • MARCH 5th

Scrub all that stuff I wrote yesterday. *Second* day on the checkout and check *this* out, baby! I think I'm in luuuuurve!! This guy! Oh my god, is he totally lush, or what? And he clearly chose *my* checkout when there were several others with much smaller queues! Why? Was it fate? Was it that he somehow sensed that I and I alone could fill the aching, bottomless void at the very core of his being? Or was it because I was staring at him like a complete divvy with my tongue hanging out, dribbling all down my nylon coat? I might as well have had a sign pointing at my mouth, saying 'Snog here'!! How can I

22

describe this guy in one word? Hmm, let's see. Sex-on-a-stick-drop-dead-gorgeous just about covers it, I think! And he's obviously single! Well he must be. He bought a chicken tikka masala and rice which clearly said 'serves one' on the packet, as well as an individual meat pie and a small carton of milk. Call me Sherlock Holmes but this guy is most definitely *available*, baby! Must phone Meera and tell her! That's if I can get through, of course. That girl is never off her mobile!!

Seb • MARCH 7th

So it's our school's turn to be inspected by Ofsted, is it? Great. That's all we need. A bit more meaningless red tape. A bit more pointless and time-consuming bureaucracy cooked up by a bunch of sheep in suits with nothing better to do? And where *do* they get these names from anyway? No doubt there's some lowly worker-droid in an office somewhere whose job it is to dream them up! For real! You know, like a Department Of Stupid Names or something! I mean come on, man. Surely they can do better than that, can't they? Ofsted? Sounds more like a place in Belgium to me, dude!

Steven • **MARCH 9th**

Sheer XTC. Walked home with Clare 2day. Talked all way. Clare, not me! Felt gr8 though. 4got I live on other side of town. Didn't matter. Clare said C U 2morrow. Got bus home. Eggenchips 4 T.

Clare • **MARCH 11th**

Is it too late to switch A levels, I wonder? Aye, probably. Honestly, if I'd known that Biology was going to be as inhumane as this, I'd never have done it. Mr Martin's only gone and brought in these two wee rats, hasn't he? Dead cute they are too. Apparently we're going to be observing their behavioural patterns as part of some ongoing scientific experiment. Aye and then what'll happen once they've served their purpose and outlived their usefulness? I expect they'll be murdered and dissected in cold blood! How totally gross and barbaric is that? Well I tell you, as a long-standing vegetarian and active proponent of animal rights, that is definitely not on! That is *so* not going to happen! I mean, you only have to look at them to know that *they* know. It's like they're somehow already resigned to their fate and are just counting down the days. One of them just kind of scitters about the cage willy-nilly like he's doing this

24

funny wee dance. Aye, Ratboy Slim I call him. And the other one just lets out this piercing, tuneless kind of wail, like a particularly nasty car alarm. I call that one Bratney Spears.

Craig • MARCH 13th

OK, so now I've got a problem. Well, I mean, I've got loads of problems. It's just that now I've got a brand spanking new one to go with all the others! The thing is, who do I talk to about it? You know, if I'm going to start communicating and all that. Who can I tell? Well, who can I trust to keep their traps shut, more like? It's a little bit delicate. Not *that* kind of delicate, by the way. Not spots on the bum kind of delicate. The thing is . . . come on, Craig! Communicate! The thing is . . . I'm being unfaithful to Mandy! Phew, there, I've said it! I feel better already. By the way I don't mean I'm actually, you know, *being* unfaithful. But I am being, well, *mentally* unfaithful I suppose you could call it. With this new student teacher we've got! Miss Dubois she's called. Well, Mademoiselle Dubois actually. She's French. On a kind of exchange thing. I'd certainly like to exchange things with her anyway. The way she says my name in that sexy French accent! Makes me go all funny. I just hope Meera hasn't noticed, what with her and Mandy being best friends and everything. After all, girls talk about stuff, don't they? Well, according to *Men Are From Margate, Women Are From Vauxhall* they do, anyway.

Meera • MARCH 15th

Hey, guess what? Mandy's head over heels in lust!! I've never seen her like this before! She's just floating around with this dumb grin on her face all the time! It's like what's-his-face, you know, the guy with the little bow and arrow . . . yeah, Cupid, has been using her for target practice or something. It's great. I'm really happy for her. Actually I'm looking forward to seeing this guy. If he's half as drop-dead gorge as Mandy reckons, then he must be really something! Apparently he keeps coming into Safebury's and making a beeline for her checkout. It hasn't got past the 'Do you have a loyalty card and would you like any cash back?' stage yet, but according to Mandy, there's been some serious eye contact! But that's OK. Me and Seb have been going out for over a month now and we still haven't even kissed! Actually I'm getting a bit fed up of waiting to be honest. Maybe he doesn't fancy me? But I'm not that horrendous, am I? And even if I was, why does he keep coming round for more 'French revision'? Hey, talking about French, we've got this new student teacher, Miss Dubois. *Ooh la la, elle est très jolie, n'est ce pas?* How Craig can read anything on the board is a complete mystery. He spends the entire lesson with his eyes popping out of his head!

Seb • MARCH 17th

Why are all the teacher-droids getting so hot and bothered about this Ofsted inspection thing, dude? They're all totally freaking out about it! You hear it when you pass the staffroom. You hear it when you pass a couple of them in the corridor. Seems to be this season's hot topic of conversation in Teacherland. But I just don't get it at all. So a bunch of suits with a bunch of clipboards are going to hang around school for a week and write a report, are they? So what? Big deal. See how they like it. I mean we get reports written about us all the time, don't we? And do we moan about it? Yeah, OK, so I used to moan about it. But then I used to moan about everything! But that was then and this is like, you know, totally now, man. Now I happen to think that there's no point banging on about something you can't control. It's a waste of energy. Yeah, energy that could be channelled into something else. Like an ongoing quest to become a seemingly-conventional-on-the-outside-but-actually-quite-subversive-on-the-inside head boy next year, for instance. Or more crucially, an ongoing quest to bring Hardcore-Speed-Opera to the masses! Talking of which man, my trusty decks await. There's some seriously banging work to be done!

Mandy • MARCH 18th

Dreamboy came into the shop today! Again!! I saw him wandering about, pretending to take an interest in the frozen veg. But all the time he was sneaking furtive glances in my direction and waiting till I was free. It was so obvious. Hey, I know the score, baby! What am I? Some kind of Reality Virgin? Anyway there he was, looking dead lush as usual. And there I was, on the point of grabbing the tannoy and calling 'Top Totty, checkout five, price check!!' when who should appear in front of me, with a right old trolleyful, but Steven flipping Stevens! Actually he's a funny bloke, old Steven. Nearly everything he bought was a cleaning product of some description! Anyway by the time I'd finished doing him, Dreamboy had gone. Yeah, cheers Steven. I owe you one, mate!

Steven • MARCH 19th

Time 2 get 2 work. Time 4 sum serious spring-cleaning. All-out war on bacteria. Gr8 new stuff. Eradic8s all known germs. Dead! Saw Mandy in Safebury's. Seemed a bit miffed 4 sum reason. Mustevbeen sumthing I didn't say.

Clare • MARCH 21st

Whoa! Time to cut down on the TV consumption or what? Why else do I keep expecting my parents to suddenly leap up from the table and break into a cheesy song and dance routine in the middle of breakfast, like they do on the adverts? Let's face it though, there's more chance of Steven Stevens becoming an after-dinner speaker than there is of that happening! The thing is, we're not exactly morning people. Mind you, come to think of it, we're not exactly afternoon or evening people either! But mornings? Forget it! We just sit there, staring morosely at our Wheaty Pops or, in the case of my father, sit

29

there, with a newspaper where his face should be. At least I assume it's my father. It could be anybody behind there. He never says anything. At least Mum and I occasionally grunt at each other, even if it doesn't usually amount to much more than 'Pass the milk' or 'You're going to be late for school'. Actually there's no chance of me being late for school. I tell you, school comes as a bit of light relief after Breakfast With The McCluskeys! I can't get out of the door quick enough. And for some reason, just lately the atmosphere's been even worse than usual. And believe me, that's saying something!

Craig • MARCH 22nd

Got my trial with Rovers coming up in a month or so. It's going to be a complete waste of time, I just know it is. I flunked with City. Why should things be any different with Rovers? I don't think I'm any better now than I was then. If anything I'm probably a bit worse. Yes OK, so I might still be the best player in the school team, but that's a bit like being a whatsit in a whatsit, isn't it? You know, a big fish in a small pond? It's no big deal. My granny could get a game in our school team. In fact she might have to this weekend if our centre half isn't over the flu in time! I suppose I ought to get practising a bit more anyway. I've really let myself go since Mandy and I have been going out. Well, kind of going out anyway. Yeah, and that's another thing. I've only gone and told my sisters about me and Mandy, haven't I? That was a major mistake, I just know it was! But what could I do? They just never let up taking the mickey out of me. Why haven't I got a girlfriend and all that. So I thought, Right, I'll tell them! So I did. Actually it was brilliant. Shut them up completely. Yeah, for about three seconds. Then all of a sudden it was 'Ooooooh! Craigy's got a girlfriend! Craigy's got a girlfriend!' You just can't win, can you? Good job I didn't tell them about Miss Dubois as well!

Meera • MARCH 24th

Is it me, or are things generally getting weirder and weirder round here? Dad's been going on and on about Seb lately. You know, what a nice young man he is and all that, and when is he coming round to do some more French revision? (*Il arrive à huit heures*, by the way.) I mean, it doesn't seem that long ago since Dad was trying to get me married off to some complete stranger on the other side of the world. And now? Well, I'm not saying he's trying to get me married off to Seb or anything, but he's certainly not discouraging me from seeing him. I just don't get it. Dad and I aren't supposed to get on. We're supposed to argue all the time. I'm supposed to hate him. I'm a sulky teenager going through 'that difficult stage', for goodness sake! What's gone wrong? Why's Dad being so flipping nice and reasonable all of a sudden?! I tell you, it's just not normal.

Seb • MARCH 24th

Just got back from Meera's. Had a bit of a ding-dong, dude. Bummer. Didn't want to. It just kind of happened. Not that it was like, you know, vicious or anything, but it was a definite ding-dong, dude! Things were a bit odd as soon as I arrived basically. Meera was being decidedly uncool and sarky, which isn't like her at all. I'd hardly got in the door and she was asking me if I'd sooner go and hang out with her old man and watch the football, which I thought was well weird. Why would I want to do that? I mean, her old man's all right and all that. Yo! Big up Mr Kohli! Respect due! But you know, call me old-fashioned, it's Meera I'm going out with, not him! And besides, I hate football. Things went rapidly downhill from there. Check this out, right? Meera thinks I don't dig her! You know, physically and that. She said that if I did, I would have at least tried to kiss her by now. Then she started apologising and blaming it on Venus being in Aquarium or something and I told her that I thought all that horoscope stuff was like, you know, total garbage, man. Yeah, so then she started crying. I thought, Whoops, better offer some support here, dude. A bit of, you know, emotional solidarity and all that. So I started crying too. Hey, nothing wrong with that, man! Nothing wrong with being in touch with your female side. Just as long as you don't start getting, you know, *too* girly, you know what I'm saying? Anyway, at that moment Meera's dad came in to see if we wanted a cup of tea. I made my excuses and left.

Meera • MARCH 25th

Ohmygodohmygodohmygod!! Some weekend this has been! Talk about turbulent! For a start, Dad was in a huff with me last night! Can you believe it? In a huff with *me*! And why? I'll tell you. For upsetting Seb, that's why! Me upsetting him! Never mind the fact that I was clearly upset too! His own daughter! His own flesh and blood! Oh no, it was all poor little Seb and what had

I said to him? I was gobsmacked, I really was. So gobsmacked, in fact, that I didn't know what to say. In the end I just made something up. Said we'd been role-playing a scene in French and that we'd got a bit carried away! Don't think he believed me though. Actually I don't really care to be honest. Because things have moved on since then. And how! The doorbell went earlier on tonight and there was Seb, standing on the front step with a bunch of flowers and this stupid grin on his face. And guess what? He just grabbed me and kissed me right there and then! Phwoar! Some kiss it was too! How could I be angry with him? How could I resist? Exactly! So I didn't!

Clare • MARCH 27th

See all that stuff I wrote about school being a bit of light relief compared to my family? I take it all back! Why? Because today we had the most tedious talk from Brewster in the entire history of tedious talks from Brewster. EVER! Even worse than the one when he spent two hours lecturing us about the importance of good time-keeping, ironically making us all late for our next lessons! It was all about the Ofsted inspection. Need I say more? I mean, come on! We're talking Yawn

City, Illinois. We're talking mind-numbingly, watching-paint-dryingly dull! And I mean, it's not as if it's happening soon either. It's still a good couple of months away. My god, if the Head's this obsessed now, what's he going to be like nearer the time? Anybody would think it was important, or served a vaguely useful purpose or something! Now a team of inspectors who came to your house and spent a week carrying out checks and scrutinising you and your family? That would be useful! Aye, Ofhome you could call it!

Mandy • MARCH 28th

Still haven't heard from my alleged agent yet. Typical bloke, eh? You give them your phone number and that's the last you ever hear from them! Seriously though, how much longer will I have to wait? How much longer can I keep telling myself that it's still 'early days'? Well I've been thinking. And not just about Dreamboy either! (Though now I come to mention it, he was in the store Saturday and Sunday, looking totally god-like as usual! What is that aftershave he uses? Snog *Pour Homme*, or something?) No, I've been thinking that maybe it's time to take things into my own hands. Grab the bull by the horns, as it were! If fame and fortune ain't gonna come knocking at my door just yet, find out where it lives and knock on *its* door instead! What am I on about? I'll tell you. You know that programme on the telly? The one where a bunch of people come and do up your house for nothing? 'Rearranging Rooms'? Well I'm going to get in touch. See if they'll come and rearrange my room! Well why not? My room's an absolute nightmare. It needs rearranging big-time! Yeah, but more importantly, it'll get me on the telly, won't it?! Ta-daaa!! Simple, eh? Agents? Who needs 'em?!

Steven • MARCH 29th

3 months since last made list. No longer feel need 2 communic8 through medium of graphs! Well medium/large anyway! Just joking! (1st joke 4 2 years, 3 months, 12 days. Will 1ders never cease?) Spagbol 4 T.

Craig • MARCH 30th

Looks like it might be coming up to crunch time with me and Mandy. So OK, we've been playing it cool, but things have been getting practically arctic just lately. Oops, I've just thought. Maybe word's got back to

Mandy about me and Miss Dubois! But I mean it's only an imaginary affair! Surely there's no harm in that, is there? After all, the wrinklies are always telling us to use our imaginations. Always droning on about the olden days and how, back in the 70s, they made their own entertainment and how there were no such things as Playtendos and Gamestations, blah blah blah. Change the flipping record, Grandad! It's the 21st century now, in case you hadn't noticed! Blimey, I came over all Seblike for a second there. Where was I? Oh yeah. Me and Miss Dubois. Maybe it's time to imagine that I dump her? Yeah, maybe that's what I should do. Mind you, it'd be a real shame. I haven't even imagined that we've kissed yet! I'm still an imaginary virgin! How sad is that?

Clare • MARCH 31st

If I had a pound for every time someone's said, 'Oh, so you're a vegetarian. Do you eat fish?' to me, I'd probably have about, ooh let me see, £150 by now! Aye and that's just this week! I mean, do these people go to Stupid College or what? They're so clueless it's scary! I used to take the time to try to explain. You know, give them a bit of the old Fundamentalist Veggie

Manifesto. But I don't bother any more because they never listen anyway. They wait patiently till I've finished and then they say, 'Do you eat chicken? Because that's not really meat, is it? What about tuna? What about turkey? What do you eat at Christmas, then? Lettuce? Ha ha!' I mean, come on!! We're not living in the 20th century any more! God, what must it have been like when my mum first announced she was going veggie?! Bet you could have heard a pinto bean drop! Talk about rocking the gravy boat! But that was back in the Dark Ages! When men were men and the only people who didn't eat meat were limp-wristed-tree-hugging-whale-loving-lentil-worshipping-open-toed-sandal-wearing-bearded freaks! Surely things have moved on since then, haven't they? I mean, loads of people are veggie now. It's no big deal. So how come, when I have the sheer audacity to ask if the soup's made from veggie stock, do I still get gawped at as if I've just stood up on the table and taken all my clothes off? Huh?

APRIL

Meera • **APRIL 1st**

Ohmygodohmygod. I *so* hate April Fool's Day . . . No I don't! Ha ha ha!! April Fool!! Actually I really do hate it. Why people persist with all those screamingly unfunny practical jokes and oh so hilarious 'pranks' is beyond me. All those spoof stories in the papers and on the news. What's the point? When Mandy called me this morning and told me she was thinking about giving up blokes for Lent and becoming a nun, the first thing I did was check out the calendar! Even Dad tried to get me and it's definitely not like him to joke about anything. Especially about money! Yeah, he said he was really disappointed at how small my mobile bills were and he'd happily pay two or three times as much! Nice one, Dad! Really had me going there for a minute! And the thing is, it's not like I don't have a sense of humour or anything, because I do. Well I must do. I go out with Seb, don't I? Talking of Seb, he's coming round tonight. Says he's got some 'well banging tunes' he wants to play me. Frankly I don't care if they're 'well banging' or not, just as long as we have another snog like the other night! Hey, maybe I could get Dad back. Tell him that Seb's asked me to marry him! Now that *would* be funny!

Seb • APRIL 2nd

Question, dude. How come Dennis, my biological (or 'diabolical' as I call him when I'm feeling particularly satirical) father, a guy who was a punk back in '77 (hey, I've seen the photos and they're awesome!) and who was at the Snot Gobblers' first ever gig (no more brackets, man, this sentence is getting seriously complicated), can now have mellowed to the point where he's positively gagging for the new Cliff De Burgh album to be released? Sorry but I just don't get it. I mean, do your taste buds just stop developing when you get to 21 or something? What happens after that? You just live out your last few remaining years wearing sensible knitwear, washing your car and pottering round garden centres! Yeah, and listening to Cliff De Burgh albums! So what if you can hear the words? From what I can tell, most of the words are about supermarkets and the various types of mortgage that are currently available! I mean, we are talking seriously sad here, dude. I tell you, I feel like saying, 'Look, Dennis man, it's not too late. It doesn't have to be this way.' I mean, look at Meera's dad. Yeah OK, so the guy must be at least 40, but those Eastern beats he was playing last night were well hard! In fact it's given me an idea for a slight change of musical direction. Yeah, Hardcore-Speed-Garage-Bhangra!! Right here! Right now! Check it out, man!!

Craig • APRIL 4th

OK, so I've given Miss Dubois the imaginary heave-ho. It wasn't easy, but it had to be done. We were sitting in the park, having an imaginary chat and I just came out and said it. Told her that I had to stop thinking about her, before someone else got hurt. She took it surprisingly well really. I'd like to think we can still be imaginary good friends. At least now I can concentrate on practising hard for the trial with Rovers, which is what I should be doing. If only I hadn't told my flipping sisters that I'd got a girlfriend! I only did it to shut them up. Yeah, unfortunately though, it's had the complete opposite effect! They won't stop going on about it. Who is she? When am I going to bring her home? Have we <u>done it</u> yet? Yeah right. Like I'm going to tell them! Even if we had. Which we haven't. Obviously.

Mandy • APRIL 5th

How bizarre. Craig's asked me if I want to go round to his place sometime! But why would I want to do that? Don't we see enough of each other at school or something? What would we talk about anyway? Let's face it, I don't know the first thing about football. Well, apart from the fact that Darren Peckham is undoubtedly Grade A Totty of the highest order and can come round to my place any day of the week to practise his free kicks! Woooof!! Anyway, I kind of said yeah, all right then, but only because I couldn't think what else to say. Perhaps he wants to talk about something other than football? Not terribly likely, I know, but then stranger things have happened. No, on second thoughts, stranger things probably haven't happened. Maybe he wants some advice? You know, about girlie stuff or something? I mean, I don't suppose he can talk to his sisters about that kind of thing. Sweet guy, Craig. Dead insecure though. Personally what I reckon he really needs is a girlfriend. Well, maybe not a girlfriend, but definitely a damn good snog! Not that I'm offering, mind you! Uh-oh, I've just thought. Maybe he thinks me and him . . . nah, don't be ridiculous, Mandy. What have I ever done to give him that impression? Well, apart from ramming my tongue down his throat that time, ha ha! Blokes, eh? What are they like?

Steven • APRIL 7th

Found gr8 new website 2night. Floor.com. All about floors. History of floors. Philosophy of floors. Types of floors. Wooden floors, tiled floors, stone floors. Even 4um for fellow floor fans to chat called floorum! Good 1! Never thought 2 much about floors b4. But we all need them. Think about it.

Meera • APRIL 9th

Why doesn't Seb ask me round to his place for a change? We've been seeing each other for nearly two months now and he's never once suggested it. Why? Do I embarrass him? Does he think I'd make a complete divvy of myself in front of his parents or something? Well, that's assuming he actually has parents of course! You never hear him talking about them. Perhaps he hasn't even told them about me? Perhaps he's afraid that they wouldn't approve? Well, whatever it is, I think I deserve to know. I mean, I really like Seb and everything. We've got a good thing going on. Well, when I can actually understand him we have! It's just that I'm getting a bit fed up with him always coming round to my place. My parents know fine well we're not revising French any more. Not that we ever did, mind you! But the annoying thing is, they're being really cool about it. They're always going on about Seb, like he's some kind of golden boy or something. Like the sun shines out of him. Which was nice for a while. But now? Well, it's really starting to get on my nerves! Hmm, only one thing for it. A quick call to Psychic Sue's Astro Chatline! Guaranteed to resolve those tricky personal dilemmas we all find ourselves in. Well, that I find myself in, anyway! Only 50p a minute off-peak too! Bargain or what?

Saw Meera at school today. Well, she saw me. Marched straight up and demanded to go back to my place! I said, 'What, you mean right now, Meera man?' You know, thinking (not unnaturally) that she wanted my body big-time and everything. I said, 'Because now isn't really a great time, baby, what with double English just about to start.' Anyway it turned out she didn't want my body big-time after all. Not just then, anyway. Turned out she wanted to go to my place for a change and, you know . . . MEET MY PARENTS!!! Well, that's cool. She was going to have to meet them at some point, I suppose. Yeah, that point being ONCE HELL HAS FROZEN OVER, DUDE!!!! I mean, come on! How can I possibly subject Meera to An Audience With Dennis And Marjorie – The World's Most Boring Couple, and still expect her to go out with me afterwards? I couldn't do it, man. I care for Meera way too much. Anyway, I said I'd think about it, even though I just had! So then she started going on about how now was a good time because Mars is rising and the moon's transiting through Gemini or something! I never did find out what that's got to do with meeting Dennis and Marjorie, because at that point her phone rang and that was the end of the conversation basically.

Clare • APRIL 12th

Can't wait for the Easter holidays, if only so we don't have to listen to old Brewster droning on about this flipping Ofsted thing any more! Well, not for a couple of weeks anyway. Honestly, he's got some nerve. Suggesting there might be some kind of 'incentive' to 'do our bit' and make sure the school scores highly. 'Incentive'? What exactly does he mean by that, I wonder? Because I tell you what, that sounds like a bribe to me! You know, you scratch our back and we'll scratch yours and all that. Oh gross! The thought of scratching Brewster's back! I think I'm going to be sick!

Craig • APRIL 14th

Mandy Mandy
Rhymes with Gandhi
True but not
Especially handy.

Mandy • APRIL 15th

I may have to cut this short any second now and go for a lie down. Supermarketman came into the shop today, not once, but twice!! Oh my god! He is so gorgeous!

And sooo mature. Well he should be. He must be at least twenty-five!! Honestly, what am I like?! But the way he looked at me! Woooof!! If ever a look was loaded with hidden meaning, that was the one! And if you think I'm making this stuff up, or that I've been reading too many Barbara Collins books, think again. I was on '9 items or less' and he must have had at least thirty things in his trolley. What did he do? Go to another checkout? No, he just divided his stuff into separate baskets and came past me four times! Now if that's not true lust, I don't know what is! I swear he was on the point of asking me out and what happened? Craig turned up with some sprouts and a packet of Rich Tea biscuits and asked me if I'd go round to his place next week sometime! *That*'s what happened! Aaaaaaargh!!!!!

Steven • APRIL 16th

Found another gr8 website. Doublename.com. 4 people with same 1st + last names. Like me, Steven Stevens! i.e. 4 people with unimagin8ive parents. Like me, Steven Stevens! 4 people with nothing better 2 do. Like me, Steven Stevens! Not 4getting John Johns, Joan Jones, Tim Timms, Barry Barry + any1 else who doesn't know me. Baked pot8o 4 T. TV. Bed.

Honestly, you should see the number of kids who come to school by car. And I don't just mean the ones who get dropped off by their parents either. I mean the ones who actually drive to school! Aye, in their own cars!! It's unbelievable, it really is! And it's not like they're old bangers or anything. Some of them are dead flash and brand new! Much better than most of the teachers' anyway! And I mean, apart from the obvious adverse environmental implications (basically, if everyone walked or cycled to school there'd be a fraction of the traffic on the road and a fraction of the pollution, not to mention all the fuel that would be saved!) how on earth can they afford to buy them? I'll tell you. They can't afford to buy them. But Mummy-wummy and Daddy-waddy can! Which I personally think is totally and morally wrong, by the way! How can you possibly justify spending that kind of money on a car for little Johnny or Jenny when it could be spent on something much more worthwhile or useful? It's obscene, that's what it is. As for my mummy-wummy and daddy-waddy? Well, judging by what I could pick up of last night's muffled 'conversation' they seem to be getting on as well as they ever do, i.e. not very.

Meera • APRIL 18th

Four more days before we break up for Easter. And then? Well, hopefully two weeks of mucking about with Mandy, catching up on some serious reading (check out the pic of Leo De Janeiro on the front of this month's *Not Quite 19*!) and, who knows, maybe a spot of tonguenastics with Seb? But that's really up to him. Either he asks me back to his place soon or . . . well, we'll just have to see, won't we? But I'm not going to put up with it much longer. Mandy thinks it's totally outrageous. She's even offered to have a word with Seb about it, but I think I'll sort this one out myself! Hey, no time like the present. I'll call him right now!

Seb • APRIL 18th

Yo! Diary! Meera just called. But check this out! Some sixth sense told me it was her and what she wanted. Somehow I just knew. So I pulled this stunt, right? I'm not proud about it or anything. I mean, she's my woman, man, but she caught me on the hop. Didn't have any choice, dude. Couldn't think what else to do basically. And besides, I'm doing it for her own good. Let's face it, there are things lurking out there, man. Things you don't want to know. Things you're better off staying clear of. Yeah, like my parents for instance. They're losing it big-time, baby. Marjorie's currently crocheting a map of Belgium and Dennis has started videoing the news and watching it the next day! How can I possibly take Meera to meet these people? No, she must be protected at all costs, man. Even if that means a little subversive skulduggery from time to time, you know what I'm saying? Anyway, luckily I was like, you know, thinking on my feet and seriously alert mentally as usual. Sorted it basically. Got away with it this time, but it was a close call, dude.

Meera • APRIL 18th

What does Seb take me for? Stupid or something? Fancy pretending to be the answerphone like that when he heard it was me! So pathetic! And sooo obvious! All that 'Er, I'm too radical to come to the phone right now, maaan, but you know, you can like, leave a message after the beep if you want, but if you don't want to, hey that's cool. Respect! Beeeep'! So I left a message. I said, 'Hi Seb, it's me. I just want to know when you're going to invite me round to your place and introduce me to your parents? See you tomorrow. Oh, that's if you're not being too radical, of course.' And then I put the phone down. That should make him think. Hope so anyway.

Craig • APRIL 19th

Why are my parents walking round with these stupid grins on their stupid faces and being so feely-touchy and kissy with each other all of a stupid sudden? Are they actually trying to make me feel even worse or something? Don't they realise how insensitive they're being? Why don't they just take out a full-page advert in the paper and be done with it? *OUR SON CRAIG MIGHT NOT BE DOING IT BUT WE ARE!!!* Anyway it's disgusting at their age. Shouldn't be allowed. But it is. In fact, according to *Men Are From Margate, Women Are From Vauxhall* it's actually quite common for couples to continue enjoying 'a healthy s– life' well into their 30s! Even longer! God, right now I'd settle for any kind of s– life. I wouldn't care if it was healthy or not!

Mandy • APRIL 20th

Rumour has it there's a new guy starting school after Easter! Hmmm. Rumour also has it that this guy could well turn out to be a quality piece of trouser! Not that

I'm interested of course! Let's face it, it's only a matter of time before Supermarketman and I get down to some serious mouth-to-mouth resuscitation, if you know what I mean! Still, it's something to look forward to when we get back, isn't it? After all, there's no harm in looking! Put it this way. Just because you browse, doesn't mean to say you have to buy! Oh and talking about after the holidays . . . I'm not sure if this is a wind-up or not . . . but we're supposed to be getting this caravan brought in so that the Ofsted inspectors have their own space to work and relax in! Sounds a bit wacky, I know, but apparently they have to have somewhere that's off-limits to non-Ofsted people and there isn't a spare room in the school. Still, it'll make a nice change from snogging behind the bike sheds, I suppose! Ha ha!!

Steven • **APRIL 22nd**

Best website yet! Just typed 'household hygiene', pressed 'search' + bingo! Fluff.com. The ultim8 guide 2 spring-cleaning! Handy household hints 4 stain removal, latest product news + everything U ever needed 2 no about hoovers! Fascin8ing. Oh and not 4getting the inev8able 4um 4 those who wish 2 chat on-line! Gr8 2 no I'm not alone. Fishenchips 4 T. TV. Wrote Clare's birthday card. Wrote this. Bed.

Clare • APRIL 23rd

This is unbelievable! Absoflippinglutely unbelievable!! After all I said about kids driving to school, what do my folks go and buy me for my birthday? A CAR!!!!! Aaaaarrrrggghh!!!!! Talk about moral dilemma!! Aye, and whilst you're all doing that I'll be going for a wee drive!! Moral dilemma? Moral dilemma my arm!! This is so amazing! My very own set of wheels!! I mean, I'll have to get lessons and do my test first and everything, but after that? You won't see me for dust! Just think of all the places I'll be able to go to. I'll even be able to drive to demos and stuff! Oh man, this is just the best thing that's ever happened to me! When my parents took me outside and chucked me the keys I just stood there for a moment, totally gobsmacked and then started bawling my eyes out. Mum and Dad stood there, grinning. Then, in an unprecedented display of public emotion (well, not exactly public, but it was in front of me) Dad put his arm round Mum and gave her a wee peck on the cheek! Hey, just a thought, but I wonder if this is what they've been bickering about all this time? Whether or not to get me a car? Hmm, and I wonder if it would be ungrateful if I . . . Nah, I couldn't. Could I? It's just that, well, red's a really nice colour and everything but I've actually always fancied a metallic blue one. I wonder if it's too late to swap?

Seb • APRIL 24th

Whoa, this is getting pretty heavy, man. Now Meera's dad has started dropping hints about him and Mrs Kohli wanting to meet Dennis and Marjorie and inviting them round for tea and stuff! Are they crazy? What do they want to do that for? I tried changing the subject by talking about music. I even suggested me and Mr K meet up and do a bit of mixing and DJ-ing sometime. Told him about the Hardcore-Speed-Garage-Bhangra. Said we should work on a few beats and tunes together. As a matter of fact, Mr K seemed well up for it. Meera didn't seem very pleased though, and was more keen on changing the subject back to my parents! Yeah, nice one, Meera man! Big up!! Luckily I was thinking on my feet again. Told them that Dennis and Marjorie were likely to be out of circulation for a while. The moment passed. Got away with it again. But it was another close call, dude!

Meera • APRIL 24th

So Seb's parents have been struck down with a rare and highly contagious form of tropical disease and have to be kept in strict isolation for the next six months, eh? Well I suppose that's the risk you take when you travel to exotic and far-flung places like they do. Where was it they went last summer? Oh that's right. Torquay. Actually I think they're being even more adventurous and going to Wales this year! That's if they've recovered in time, of course. Funny how Seb seems to have avoided being infected too, but then hey, what do I know about these things? I'm just a stupid girlie, aren't I? But you know, I think I might just risk it and pop round anyway. See if there's anything I can do for them. Take them some fruit, or maybe offer to go to the shops or something? I mean, it's the least I can do, isn't it?

Seb • APRIL 25th

OK, so now I've told Meera that I was adopted when I was three days old. So what? Drastic measures were called for, dude! She just turned up on the doorstep. Dennis had got there before I could and by the time I arrived on the scene it was already too late. Meera had made the fundamental error of complimenting Dennis on his roses and Dennis had launched straight into a list of preferred fertilisers! I could see Meera's eyes just beginning to glaze over. That's when I knew I had to do something and fast! It was only a matter of time before he offered to show her his cactus collection! It just came to me in a moment of blinding clarity, man. I ushered Meera out of harm's reach and told her there was something she should know. Told her Dennis and Marjorie weren't my real parents at all. Told her my real parents had been astronauts and had been lost in space whilst on a top secret mission to Mars. I must admit, I was pretty impressed with myself for coming up with an explanation like that. Yeah, unfortunately though, Meera wasn't. She just looked at me and said, 'Come on, Seb, surely you can do better than that, can't you?' I said, 'Sorry, Meera man, I'll see what I can do.' We smiled at each other, so I think everything's cool. Then we went back over to Dennis. He hadn't even noticed we'd gone. He was still going on about fertilisers.

Meera • APRIL 26th

Why couldn't Seb just have been more honest with me instead of coming out with all that garbage about tropical diseases and missions to Mars? Why couldn't he

56

just have said, 'Look, Meera, the reason I don't want to introduce you to my parents is because they embarrass me'? I mean, I could have related to that, couldn't I? After all, my parents embarrass me! All parents are embarrassing. That's life. It's in the contract. I'll probably be embarrassing too when I'm a parent. You know, complaining loudly in shops and stuff. It's what they do! I was just curious to meet them. It seemed like a fairly natural step to take if this relationship is to move forward. Doesn't mean to say I suddenly want to move in, or be their best mate or anything. I just wanted to say, 'Hi, I'm going out with your son,' that's all. What's so weird about that? Actually I thought Seb's dad seemed really nice. I honestly had no idea there were so many different kinds of fertiliser!

Mandy • APRIL 26th

Well whaddya know? Just got a call from this researcher guy on 'Rearranging Rooms'!! I'd almost forgotten about it. It's ages since I wrote to them. He wants to come round in a couple of weeks to check the place over. Yeah, and check me over too! Woooof! What am I like? Actually he said he'd been trying to get through for ages. Yeah, well that's because I've been talking to

Meera for the past two hours, isn't it? Well, strictly speaking she's been talking to me. More Seb trouble. I felt like saying, 'Girlfriend, Seb *is* trouble!' But I didn't. I just let her get it all off her chest. I think I might have even nodded off at one point. Well I must have. How could she have been talking about relationships one minute and missions to Mars the next? Or maybe it was just something to do with astrology and horoscopes and stuff? God, I dread to think what that girl's mobile bills are like! Having said that though, perhaps it's time for me to get a mobile too? I mean, after all, I am on the threshold of becoming a major media personality, aren't I? Well, maybe anyway!

Craig • **APRIL 28th**

Mandy's finally coming round tomorrow. That should hopefully shut my sisters up once and for all. Well, I don't know about once and for all, but for a while anyway. No doubt they'll find something else to take the mickey about soon enough. I've got my trial with Rovers this weekend (wow, two things happening in less than a week! Must be some kind of record for me) and just suppose . . . not very likely, I know, but just suppose it goes OK and they want me to sign! It'll be all

'Oooh, Craigy's going to be a footballer! Craigy's going to be a footballer!' Yeah, they'd soon change their tune if Darren Peckham or Owen Michaels came round for a cup of tea though, wouldn't they? Yeah right, meanwhile back on Earth, Craig!

Mandy • APRIL 29th

Oh god, this is horrendous. I feel so awful. Not as awful as I imagine poor Craig must be feeling right now though. Where do I start? OK, well I went round to his place today, thinking he wanted to talk about something, you know, guy to girl kind of thing, or that he maybe needed some advice or something? But it seems I'd misread the situation just a teensy bit! And so had Craig! For a start he made this big thing of introducing me to his parents and his sisters. His mum went on and on about how nice it was to meet me and his dad told me Craig had obviously got great taste! I thought, Hang on, what's going on? But I didn't say anything. Not then anyway. I just kind of played along with it. Then after a while everybody made this big thing about leaving us alone and Craig's dad winked at Craig! That's when the penny really dropped! Well, not so much the penny as the entire flipping piggy-bank! As soon as they were gone Craig said we needed to talk! I thought, You're telling me we need to talk, Craigy boy! But before I could actually say anything he started going on about his trial with Rovers and what would happen to us if he ended up signing for them? I said, 'Craig, what do you mean, us?' That's when his face just, well, crumpled basically. It was awful. Poor Craig. Well, I won't say anything if he doesn't!

Craig • APRIL 30th

Roses are dead
Violets are too
Didn't follow the instructions
Did you?

MAY

Craig • MAY 1st

Mayday! Mayday! Calling all ships! Any chance of a lift? I don't care where you're going. In fact the further the better. I'll scrub the decks! I'll splice the mainbrace! Just get me out of here. Get me out of Molton Flipping Sodbury! I just can't take any more of this humiliation. If this was a boxing match it would have been stopped by now! As if discovering that you haven't really been going out with the person you think you've been going out with all this time and that in fact she fancies the pants off someone else entirely, thus almost certainly condemning you to live the rest of your life as a big girlie virgin, isn't bad enough – what do you think happened at the trial? I'll tell you. I got injured. And how did I get injured? By defying gravity to score with a spectacular overhead scissors kick? Nope. By leaping, salmon-like to head home an unstoppable bullet header? Nope. I got injured slipping down the steps of the bus before the trial even started, didn't I? Duh!! Just when you think things can't get any worse, they do!! I mean, you couldn't write this kind of stuff, could you? Well, you could I suppose, but I doubt whether anyone would believe you.

Steven • MAY 2nd

Bumped in2 Craig in town 2day. Asked if I 1ted 2 go 2 pictures sometime! I said yeah gr8! Craig = new best friend! Presume he meant go with him + not by myself? That would B s2pid! Also asked how 2 join Foreign Legion? Possibly joking? Will surf Net anyway, just in case.

Clare • MAY 3rd

You should have seen the looks I got, turning up at school today in my car! Pure unadulterated envy! Aye and that was just from the teachers! The car's still red by the way. Oh and it's called Bessy. Not sure why. She just suited it. Anyway it was fab. Shades on! Sunroof down! Radio blasting out! Pity about the L-plates and Dad sitting next to me, but then you can't have everything, can you? Talking about Dad, he and Mum are still bickering away like they're practising to go on the Terry Springer show or something! Aye, so bang goes my theory about them just arguing over the car! It was really good to be back at school by the way. Good to see Ratboy and Bratney again! I'm sure they recognised me. I can't bear to think that in a few short weeks from now they'll be whizzing round that great wheel in the sky. Well, what's left of them after they've been butchered in cold blood will be, anyway!

Seb • MAY 4th

May the 4th be with you! It's a joke, dude! May the 4th be with you! *Star Wars*? Popular film from the last century? My so-called 'parents' were well into it, man. Well they would be, wouldn't they? Yeah, along with all the other sci-fi anoraks. Got the T-shirt and most of the other merchandise too, including an Obi-Wan Kenobi egg-timer and a Darth Vader toilet-seat cover! Hey, can't wait to inherit those babies! That's another joke, by the way. Hey, just because I'm Spokesdude For

A Generation (albeit a slightly lapsed one) doesn't mean to say I can't be bitingly satirical from time to time, man, you know what I'm saying? You know, thinking about it, maybe I really was adopted at birth? Well it would all make sense, wouldn't it? How could two people as pathologically boring as (The Phantom) Dennis and Marjorie really be genetically related to somebody as crucial and happening as me? It would explain everything, wouldn't it? And thinking about it, I've never actually seen my birth certificate!

Craig • MAY 6th

Imagine your worst nightmare. Your very worst, spine-tingling, nail-biting, pants-soiling nightmare. Something so scary it makes *The Blur Witch Project* look like an episode of 'Tubbytellies'! Are you there yet? Right. Now compare it to the one I've just had and tell me you still think yours is bad! It's so vivid. I'm still shaking. It's actually quite difficult for me to even write this down. Here goes, anyway. So there I am, the oldest living virgin in Northern Europe. No, better make that the whole of Europe. I've just split up from someone I was never going out with in the first place, dumped a beautiful but strictly imaginary girlfriend, screwed up my one big chance of becoming a professional footballer and am constantly being hounded and ridiculed by my two slavering and strangely hyena-like sisters. Then, oh my god, please tell me this isn't happening, completely out of the blue my parents walk in, arm-in-arm, grinning like idiots, and announce that my mum's pregnant!!! Yeah, I know. Gruesome, isn't it? But you see that's not the really scary part. No, the really scary part is that it's not a nightmare at all! I haven't even been asleep! My mum really is pregnant! This is really happening!! Aaaarrrrggghhhh!!!!

Meera • MAY 8th

Feeling a bit wild and reckless today! Well Kosmic Kate says that because Mars is becoming more dominant in the next few weeks and because I've been going through a bit of a difficult time emotionally just lately, I should go a bit mad and pamper myself for a change! Not that things have been that difficult lately. But hey, if Kosmic Kate says they have, that's fine by me! So anyway I've bought a new phone. Wasn't going to. It just kind of happened! Well I was passing the Vodanet Warehouse and there it was in the window, practically begging me to buy it! Hey, what's a girl supposed to do? I couldn't resist it. Actually it's dead cool. Really tiny and this amazing dayglo green colour! And that's not all! I get 30 minutes of free calls a day! Well, as long as they're local and I make them between three and four in the morning. Oh and there isn't an 'r' in the month. Which there isn't at the moment! Whoa, there's some serious dialling to be done between now and the end of August! Hmm, now what am I going to do with my old phone?

Seb • MAY 8th

Yo! Diary! Check this out! Meera just called to ask if I want a phone! I said, 'But Meera man, I've got one already! What do you think I'm talking to you on right now?' Then she got the hump. Said I knew perfectly well what she meant. Actually she was right. I did know what she meant. But what would I want a mobile for, dude? Can't stand the things! Everywhere you look now someone's walking around talking on a flipping mobile! Yeah, Mobile Clones I call them. All slaves to technology. All terrified of the thought of not being contactable until they get back home. Constantly checking to see whether anybody might have called them in the last 30 seconds. I'd like to know what percentage of calls made on a mobile are truly necessary? For real! Because as far as I can see, dude, most people just use their mobiles to call someone up and tell them that they're on their mobile! I mean, what's the point of that? You hear them on the train: 'Hi, I'm on the train!' Big deal! I don't call someone up and tell them I'm in the hall, do I? You know I hate to admit this, but when it comes to the subject of mobile phones, I actually agree with my parents. Er, my adoptive parents that is, of course.

Clare • MAY 8th

There was this new guy at school today. Troy, I think his name is. I tell you, it was a job avoiding tripping over all the tongues hanging out! Pathetic really. Just because he's quite good-looking everybody goes completely ga-ga and girlie all of a sudden! OK, just because he's *very* good-looking. But that's still no reason to start acting like a bunch of vacuous Barbies, is it? I mean, no one even knows the guy yet. He might turn out to be really horrible, or a total sexist slimeball, or have a severe personal hygiene problem or something! But oh no, just because he's an absolute hunk, with a pert wee backside and piercing blue eyes the size of dustbin lids, everyone automatically assumes he's god's gift to womankind! I mean, if that isn't shallow, what is? And besides, my car's much better than his!

Mandy • MAY 8th

Well, that's the last time I pay any attention to a rumour, then. I thought this new guy was supposed to be a 'quality piece of trouser'? 'Quality piece of trouser'?! That's a gross understatement, and if I were him, I'd sue whoever said that for defamation of character! Mind you, if I were him I'd be too busy snogging myself stupid to even think about suing! We are talking 100% Unadulterated Sex God here! We are talking Total Tongue Magnet! We are talking the result of a genetic collision between Darren Peckham, Roland from Bloke-U-Like and Leo De Flipping Janeiro (who isn't, strictly speaking 'my type', but then he is male, so I suppose he is 'my type' after all, ha ha!). Thinking about it, we must have made quite a funny sight, us girls, when he walked into the common room. You could almost hear the sound of eyes popping out of heads and jaws hitting floors. And who do you think was clearly the most lust-crazed, and whimpering like a doe-eyed puppy? Yeah, old ironpants herself, Clare McCluskey!! Wonders will never cease, eh?

Steven • **MAY 9th**

Me + Craig going 2 C new Brad Depp film 2nite. Supposed 2 B dead scary. Craig said he needs cheering up. Said something had happened but that he didn't 1t 2 talk about it + did I 1t 2 go anyway? I said yeah gr8, what time? He said 8. I said fine. Early T.

Seb • **MAY 10th**

It's sad, man, it really is. There's me thinking that the chicks in my year had a bit more, you know, respect for themselves, you know what I'm saying? I mean, I certainly didn't think they'd be the types to turn to jelly the moment the first guy who doesn't resemble the back of a bus walks in through the common room door. But it seems I was wrong. (Hey, first time for everything, dude!) Not that they *all* turned to jelly, of course. Meera didn't. Obviously. Yeah OK, so technically speaking Meera wasn't actually there at the time, but even if she had been she wouldn't have! No doubt, dude! Why would she? Is she, or is she not already going out with Captain Testosterone? Besides, this guy's clearly a zero, man! Why? Well because . . . because . . . because he just is, right? And what kind of name is Troy anyway? I'll tell you what kind it is. A made up one! His real name's probably Wayne, or Nigel or something! Don't get me wrong, I'm not dissing anyone called Wayne or Nigel, you know what I'm saying? Yo! Nigel! Respect! Big up, Wayne! But Troy? That's like calling yourself Hercules, or Zeus or something, man! Totally ridiculous! Nuff said. Seb out.

Meera • MAY 10th

Phwoar! Wonder what sign Troy is, then! Not that I'm interested, of course! Well I mean I am interested, but purely from an astrological perspective. Honest! Bet he's a Leo though. He even looks like a Leo. Yeah, Leo De Janeiro!! Hmm, this sounds like a job for Psychic Sue's Astro Chatline!

Craig • MAY 12th

Can't wait to get to school these days. Not that I've suddenly gone all weird and turned into some kind of nerdy boffin or anything. I mean, school's OK, but it's not that great. No, it's dead simple. The more time I spend at school, the less time I have to spend with my parents! Oh god, the thought of Mum having another baby at her age! It's just so gross! And the way she keeps having to rush off to the toilet to be sick in the mornings! She should be grateful it's just the mornings! I feel sick whenever I think about it! In fact I'd better change the subject pretty flipping quickly! So, anyway, French was fine today. Actually it was more than fine. Miss Dubois asked me to stay behind afterwards! Well, not just me. She asked Meera too. Asked us what we thought of her?! As a teacher, of course!! (I think she's a bit worried about this Ofsted thing and how she's going to be assessed and stuff.) It's funny, because not so long ago I'd have totally gone to pieces if she'd even talked to me, let alone asked me what I thought of her! But I didn't. In fact I was dead cool. Well, coolish. Maybe I'm not quite so over our imaginary affair as I'd imagined I was. Don't think it was too obvious though.

Meera • MAY 12th

Poor Craig. One minute he was absolutely fine, the next he was a complete gibbering wreck! Almost like he'd invented his own language! Whole sentences with scarcely a recognisable vowel sound! He's obviously totally besotted with Miss Dubois. But I think that's one that's going to remain well and truly unrequited. 'Unrequited'? What is this? A Catherine Cartland novel or something? Aw, she is lovely though. I'm sure I'd fancy her if I was a bloke! Miss Dubois I mean, not Catherine Cartland! And she's a really good teacher too. I don't know what she's so worried about. If she doesn't get full marks from Ofsted then there's something seriously wrong. By the way, I wonder what this 'incentive' is? You know, if the inspection goes smoothly and we all pull together, blah blah blah? I mean, what's Brewster going to do? Buy us all a lollipop or something?

Mandy • MAY 13th

Honestly, what are me and Meera like? Anybody would think we lived on different planets, let alone go to the same school as each other! I mean, we talk practically all day long as it is. And then what's the first thing we do when we get home? Right! We phone each other up! Like tonight. We started before tea and by the time we'd finished, 'Eastside Street' was nearly over! I've talked so much I think I might have sprained my jaw!

I feel physically and emotionally drained. Yeah but the funny thing is, I couldn't tell you what we were talking about! Men, men and more men probably, ha ha!! You know it really was brilliant, Meera giving me her old mobile like that. Still, that's what friends are for, eh?

Steven • MAY 15th

Me + Craig went 2 C City 2day. 1st ever football match! It was gr8. Not so gr8 4 Craig though. City lost 3-0. Craig didn't talk all way home. Tried 2 make him feel better by not talking either. Figured that's what friends R 4. Watched 'Rearranging Rooms'. Mandy says she's going 2 B on it sumtime! Not sure whether 2 believe her. Lasagne 4 T. Bed.

Mandy • MAY 17th

Me and Meera went into town today for a spot of much-needed retail therapy. I was basically checking out possible outfits for 'Rearranging Rooms'. Well, a girl's got to look her best, you know! Particularly a girl who's hoping to make a bit of an impact on the great telly-watching public! Anyway, there we were, in Gap Connection, having a right old laugh, when who should walk in looking drop-dead gorgeous as usual? Yeah, Supermarketman! God, you should have seen him. That dazzling smile! Those steely eyes! That rippling torso! That beautiful wife! Those two little kids screaming 'Daddy Daddy Daddy!!' I couldn't believe it. I was speechless, which is well unusual for me! What a complete and utter slimeball. Giving me the big eye whenever he's by himself in Safebury's. Giving it all that single sex god looking for luuurve stuff!! And all this time he's been like, Mr Perfect with a perfect wife and 2.4 perfect children, no doubt living in a perfect house with a perfect cat and a couple of perfect goldfish!! I feel so stupid!

Meera • MAY 18th

Just called Mandy. She seems remarkably OK about it. Or if she's not, she's doing a pretty good job of sounding like she's remarkably OK about it. Mandy's amazing, she really is. I mean, if that had been me I'd have been devastated. Lusting after this guy for weeks and then suddenly finding out he's married! Men, eh? Who needs them? Ooh, that reminds me, Seb and I are going to the pictures on Saturday night. Yeah, the new Leo De Janeiro film! Not that Seb knows that yet!

Actually I don't even know what the film's called, let alone who else is in it. Or what it's about! Who cares, frankly, as long as Leo's in it and gets to take his shirt off at some point!

Clare • MAY 19th

Ratboy Slim and Bratney Spears are not going to die!! Simple as that!! Why should they? They have rights too! And the first fundamental right they have is the right to life! The right not to have their throats cut and their bodies dissected! The right not to be chucked in the bin the moment they're no longer deemed to be useful. I mean, we're not thrown away when we're no longer considered useful to society, are we? No, we're allowed to live out the rest of our days in peace and in comfort and with a degree of dignity. Aye, then we're chucked in the bin! Metaphorically speaking, of course! (Just demonstrating that not all animal activists are totally humourless!) Hmm, now the next question is, how are Ratboy Slim and Bratney Spears not going to die? Because the way I see it is this: I can either hope to persuade Mr Martin (Biology teacher/Chief Executioner) and my fellow pupils to change their minds, with a series of impassioned, heartfelt pleas and deftly honed arguments, or . . . I can just release them, basically!! It's as simple as that. It's a matter of life or, quite literally, death. So what's it to be? This sounds like a job for the Rat Liberation Front!!

Seb • MAY 21st

Dude, that is the last time I let Meera choose which film we go to see! Because that film was pants, man! I mean, there's pants and there's pants, but that was pants, man! Serious pants!! Don't get me wrong, just because I'm a guy, doesn't mean to say I only like films with Mel Willis in them and loads of explosions and car chases. Because I don't. I like films with talking and emotional depth and stuff as well. Check this out, right? I even saw a film with subtitles once! So OK, it was total garbage, but I sat through it all! Yeah, just in case any chicks got their . . . anyway I sat through it all and that's what counts, man! But *this* film? The only thing that happened as far as I could see was that this Leo De Janeiro dude lost his shirt early on and spent the next two hours wandering round looking for it. It was totally unrealistic. I mean, come on, the money that guy must make, he could easily afford a new one! Personally I don't understand what everybody sees in him anyway.

He's nothing special to look at. And anyway, I could act better than that, man! For real! I could be a movie star! No doubt, dude! It's just that I don't want to be, that's all.

Clare • MAY 21st

Just recruited Steven Stevens into the Rat Liberation Front, or RLF as it shall henceforth be known! Well I figured I could maybe do with a bit of help and moral support. Actually I did think about asking Troy, but decided against it. I mean, I know he's like, Captain Charisma and everything, and OK, I admit it, cute as hell, but I don't really know the guy yet. For all I know he might have blabbed and put the whole operation in jeopardy! So I asked Steven Stevens instead. Let's face it, if there's one person you can rely on to keep their mouth shut, it's Steven Stevens! I know that might sound a bit rotten, but let's be brutally honest for a moment: after-dinner speaking isn't exactly a career option for Steven, is it? Mind you, having said that, he's really opened up in the last few months. Well, by his own standards he has, anyway. I don't know if it's got anything to do with him and Craig being so friendly these days? You know, maybe it's given his confidence a wee boost or something? Actually I think it's really sweet the way those two are so pally.

Steven • MAY 21st

Wow! Clare's just e-mailed me + asked me to join the RLF! Said yeah gr8, Y not? Figured friends R like waiting 4 a bus. U wait ages 4-1-2 come along + then 2 come at 1ce! Defin8ly spent less time on Net since me + Craig have been friends. Down 2 just 3 hours a night. Maybe cut down even more now! 1der what RLF is anyway?

Mandy • MAY 22nd

Is it me, or have all the teachers suddenly started being really nice to us? OK, so some of them are pretty nice anyway, but what on earth's got into Duckworth? All of a sudden he's gone from grumpy old geezer to loveable uncle! Now you can actually get a question wrong without fear of getting your head bitten off, which is quite something for Duckworth, let me tell you! Call me cynical, but I don't suppose it could have anything to do with the fact that the Ofsted inspection's coming up, could it? Perhaps the teachers think that if they're extra nice to us, we might just be extra nice to them, especially when there's some bloke with a clipboard sat at the back of the class? And is it me or was today's Maths lesson exactly the same as the one we did the other day? OK, so I spent most of the lesson on the mobile to Meera, but it definitely sounded familiar! Just joking, by the way. It was only a quick call! Ha ha!!

Craig • MAY 22nd

Miss Dubois, oh Miss Dubois
Prettier than the prettiest star
How very chic and French you are
What can I say, but *ooh la la*?
Miss Dubois, oh Miss Dubois
I worship you from near and far
I thought I saw you in your car
I thought I caught a glimpse of bra.

Clare • MAY 22nd

Ratboy and Bratney's days behind bars will soon be a thing of the past, thanks to the RLF. On a given signal from its leader, Operation Ratatouille (and I have to say, I'm particularly pleased with that name) will swing smoothly into action and they'll be released into the wild, free at last to roam wherever they want. Mind you, I still reckon we could do with another member to ensure that things go exactly to plan. The question is though, who? Who can I trust to do the business and not to bottle it when push comes to shove? And what exactly are the qualities required for an operation of this nature? Well, for a start it needs to be someone level-headed and not prone to sudden irrational outbursts. So that immediately rules out Seb! Possession of a mobile phone would be a definite plus. Hmm, Mandy's just got one. Nah, too extrovert. We need someone a little less in-your-face. Someone quietly confident. Someone like Meera. In fact, someone exactly like Meera!

Steven • MAY 23rd

Thinking of becoming vegetarian like Clare. Gesture of solidarity 4 fellow RLF member. Don't know much about vegetables. Can't remember when I last 8-1. Clare says U'd B amazed what U can do with a courgette + some free-range broccoli. 1der if I could still eat chicken? Meera 1 of us now. What do we want? Rat rights! When do we want them? Now! Burgers 4 T. Watched TV. Wrote this.

Meera • MAY 23rd

Hey, so now I'm a fully fledged member of the RLF, am I? All of a sudden I feel like I'm a character in an Ingrid Blyton book! You know, like I'm in *The Fantastic Five*, or *The Secretive Six* or something! Except there's only three of us. Anyway it's all quite exciting. We're having a meeting to discuss strategies and stuff. And because it's all supposed to be dead hush-hush and undercover and all that, we're having the meeting behind the caravan. Have I mentioned the caravan before? Well, it's been brought in so that the Ofsted inspectors have a space of their own to work in and to relax in. And it's strictly off-limits to anyone else. Doesn't mean to say you can't hang around behind it though! Actually it's dead funny. Clare reckons that if anyone accidentally interrupts us, she's going to pretend she's snogging Steven Stevens! Now there's dedication for you!

Mandy • MAY 24th

So much for being on 'Rearranging Rooms' then. What a disaster that was! The researcher guy never said he was just going to turn up like that, did he? He might have given me a bit of notice. Actually he would have needed to give me at least 48 hours' notice to get the house even vaguely presentable! Honestly, it looked like it had just been hit by Hurricane Sharon or something! Not that I'm blaming Mum. If I was juggling three jobs like she is then the last thing I'd want to do when I got home would be tidy up. Talk about state of emergency though! We're talking piles of dishes and coffee mugs! We're talking pizza boxes strewn everywhere! We're talking floor totally covered in rubbish and dirty washing! And that was just my room! Ha ha! Except it wasn't very funny at the time. The guy was really sweet about it though. In fact, the guy was really sweet full stop! But no amount of eyelash fluttering from yours truly (and believe me, there was some serious fluttering going on) was going to persuade him that I was right for the programme. Frankly they could do an entire series at this place and it wouldn't make the slightest bit of difference! Oh well. Didn't want to be on anyway. Hey, maybe I should get in touch with that programme where they come and do up your garden instead? What's it called again? 'Changing Blooms'? Yeah, that's the one!

Craig • MAY 25th

Great. Just great! So now it's official. Yeah, if it wasn't already! I, Craig Glover, am totally repulsive to females of the opposite thingy. Well I mean, I must be, mustn't I? If Steven Stevens can get a snog and I can't? What other conclusion am I supposed to come to? No offence, Steven, by the way. You're my mate and everything. Not that you're ever going to read this. Well I hope not anyway! I suppose I should look for something positive to take out of this. Like it says in *Men Are From Margate*, very often things aren't quite as bad as they first appear. OK, so in my case, things are very often worse than they first appear. But thinking about it now, if Steven Stevens can get to snog someone as nice as Clare McCluskey, then there's hope for losers like me yet! There we go. I feel a lot better now!

Clare • MAY 25th

Phew, that was a bit of a close call, but I think we got away with it! Aye, only just though! Honestly, the look on Craig's face when he came round the corner and saw us! It was absolutely priceless! Mind you, the look on Steven's face was pretty priceless too! It wasn't easy either, but someone had to do it! And I couldn't very well get Meera to kiss him, could I now? I mean, word could have got back to Seb and then things could have got extremely messy! Besides, the whole security of the

RLF was at stake! All of a sudden the entire success of Operation Ratatouille was hanging in the balance! And I have to say, Steven played his part admirably. Helped make it all totally convincing. I was really proud of him. He deserves a medal! He knows it was all for the cause. He knows not to read too much into it. At least, I hope he does!!

Stephen • MAY 25th

Gnumph mmm gnnnn kabaffa babababa phoooor lammalamma furgan boobarooba mmm yeah Clare baby youandme mmmmmmm gggggggrrrrrrrrrrrr hubba hubba hubba gagagaga oooooh humpharooooobadooba yeeeeeee eaaaahhh.

Mandy • MAY 26th

You know how just about every day you hear about some new syndrome or other? Going To The Shops Syndrome, or Can't Decide What To Wear Syndrome? Or People Who Are Addicted To Syndromes Syndrome? (Otherwise known as Get A Life Syndrome!) Well I don't know if there's one called Mobile Phone Syndrome or not, but if there is, Meera's got it big-time! OK, so I like a good chinwag myself, but honestly, Meera's in another league altogether! I mean, what was she like today? That girl has got a serious problem! Well, two serious problems if you include Seb! And as it happens, our local friendly Spokesdude did feature quite heavily in the conversation. Well, I say 'conversation'. That implies we were both actually talking. I couldn't get a word in edgeways. The girl was on total verbal hyper-drive! In the end I just had to cut in and say, 'Look, Meera doll, it's half past three in the morning and I'd quite like to go back to bed now if that's OK with you. We can talk about this later on at school.' I'm not sure but I think she might have got the hump with me.

Clare • MAY 26th

This is it then. Less than 24 hours before Operation Ratatouille! And then? Freedom for Ratboy Slim and Bratney Spears!! An end to a so-called life where one day blurs imperceptibly into the next. An end to merely existing for the benefit of other, allegedly more intelligent life forms. As long as everything goes to plan of course! And there's no reason it shouldn't. We all know what to do. At a given signal from me, Meera's going to discreetly phone the school office and tell them she has to speak to Mr Martin urgently. He'll have to leave the room for a minute. And as soon as he does, I'll distract the others whilst Steven lowers the cage out of the window! Then, as soon as the lesson's over I'll nip round, grab the cage and be on my way! I'll bring it back the next day and no one will be any wiser. Of course then they'll discover that the cage is empty, but it'll just look like Ratboy and Bratney have escaped themselves! *Et voila*! One nil to the RLF!! So simple. So beautiful! What can possibly go wrong?

Steven • MAY 26th

Big day 2morrow. Operation Rata2y. Bit nervous. Never done anything like this B4. Obviously. Am mentally prepared though. Been veggie 4 nearly 6 hours now. Well, apart from bacon sandwich. Final RLF meeting 2night. Meera not there. Phoned up instead. Clare gave gr8 speech. Wished us luck. 1der if I'll get another kiss? Gnumphwoar hubba roobagurgunfurgun babababa nnnnnn. Got 2 calm down. Got 2 relax. Maybe do spot of cleaning? Some stubborn stains on kitchen unit doors.

Meera • MAY 27th

Ohmygodohmygodohmygod!! This has to be the ultimate nightmare, doesn't it? Having your mobile confiscated? How am I supposed to communicate with people now? This is so unfair!! And all because of a couple of stupid rats! OK, so you could say it was my own fault. I mean, I know I was supposed to phone the school office. I shouldn't really have phoned Mandy first. Particularly when she was halfway through double Maths. But I had to. It was totally vital. How else was I supposed to find out what happened at the end of 'Who Wants To Be Very Rich Indeed'? What was I supposed to do? Wait until break or something? Oh well, it's not as if I'll be able to phone Mandy, is it? After all, she's had her mobile confiscated as well. And it is only for a week. I guess I'll just have to live without it. Yeah right! Wonder what time the Vodanet Warehouse stays open till?

Clare • MAY 27th

Oops. That's the last time I say 'What can possibly go wrong?' OK, so the ultimate aim of Operation Ratatouille has been achieved – i.e. Ratboy Slim and Bratney Spears have been liberated. Which totally brilliant, by the way! Big up the RLF! as Seb would no doubt say. But whichever way you look at it, there's no disguising the fact that things didn't go quite as smoothly as planned! Actually that's a wee bit of an understatement. How we got away with it I'll never know! But we did. Aye, mainly thanks to Steven Stevens and no thanks whatsoever to Meera! Fancy phoning Mandy for a wee blether at such a crucial moment! I mean, Gordon flipping Bennet, vicar!! What was she thinking? Still, at least Mr Martin confiscating her mobile like that gave Steven a glimmer of an opportunity to grab the cage. And a glimmer was all he needed too, by the way. Just a pity he dropped it out of the window instead of lowering it! Oh well. Ratboy and Bratney got away, so that's the main thing, I suppose. Quite where they got away to is another matter entirely!

Mandy • MAY 28th

Blimey O'Reilly! Where do I start? There we all were, hanging out in the common room, reading, chatting or listening to music, when who should suddenly burst through the door but Mr 'Hey, call me Dave' Sissons himself! No apologies for not knocking first or making an appointment. He just launched straight into this rant about how important it is for the school to do well at Ofsted and how we should all pull our socks up if we don't want it to end in tears and how, if we're not careful, one thoughtless individual could ruin it for everyone! He said that if the person responsible owned up quickly, that would be the end of the matter and there'd be no further repercussions! We were all like, You what? What's going on? So then he told us. About the graffiti! How some complete divvy had sprayed THIS SCHOOL LIKE, TOTALLY SUCKS, MAAAAN!! all down the side of the Ofsted caravan! Well I say 'some complete divvy'. Like we don't know who did it! Naturally all heads turned to Seb. But he was like, 'Hey, what are you looking at me for, dudes? I'm like, you know, totally innocent!' I'm not sure, but I think that was the point when the rat suddenly popped out of the coffee machine. Oh yeah, and Dave fainted.

Seb • MAY 28th

Well it's nice to know who your friends are, isn't it? Even Meera thinks it was me who did the graffiti! My own girlfriend! She hasn't actually come out and said so, but I can tell she does. I tell you, I'm well insulted. It's just not my style, man. Or colour! Dayglo purple?

Whoa, Vom City, dude! OK, so I suppose I can see why they all think I might have had something to do with it. Even though I didn't! I mean, it's the sort of thing I might have done once upon a time, dude. Thinking I was being terribly anarchic and subversive and a little bit dangerous. But that was then and this is now, man! Why would I want to do it? Now, of all times? Just before Ofsted? Just before any decisions regarding, oh I don't know, let's say, who's to be head boy next year, might be taken? Anyway I told them I had nothing to do with it, basically. Yeah, and I also took the opportunity to, you know, echo Dave's sentiments about pulling our socks up and doing our bit to make sure the inspection goes well and stuff. 'Course I waited until Dave had come round again before I did it. No point doing it while he was still out cold, was there? Well I mean, you never know who might get to hear about my little speech, do you, man?

Meera • MAY 28th

'Your alleged boyfriend is sadly deluded and clearly living in Cloud Cuckoo Land if he really expects you to believe he didn't do it. What does he take you for? Stupid or something? However, with Mars, your love sign, being dominant this month, plus the fact that you currently feel dead insecure and about as attractive as the back of a Number 6 bus, you're inclined to disregard the above and give the flipping great divvy the benefit of the doubt.'

Craig • MAY 29th

Half term next week. Thank flip! No more emergency assemblies like the one today! Brewster was going absolutely ballistic, marching up and down, frothing at the mouth, ranting and raving! He reckons that if this had been Ofsted week the school would have got a complete and utter rollicking and that he'd have been out of a job. So not all bad news then! Seriously though, I thought he was going to burst a blood vessel! Particularly when the rat ran across the stage like that. But I've been thinking. I mean, it's all a bit whatsit, isn't it? A bit hypothetical? Because I mean, it isn't Ofsted week, is it? Not yet anyway. So I mean there's still time to pull our socks up and get it together and all that, isn't there? It's like City last season, needing to win their final match at United to stay up. That's what the school needs to do. Win their final match! Yeah, the only trouble is though, City lost and got relegated! Oh well.

I wonder who it was who did the graffiti anyway? Brewster says they caught someone red-handed. Well, purple-handed actually. I expect we'll find out sooner or later.

Clare • MAY 29th

Poor old Steven, eh? Talk about being in the wrong place at the wrong time! So he was caught behind the caravan with an aerosol can in his hand? It was a can of Mr Shiny for goodness sake, not paint!! All he was doing was trying to clean the graffiti off, not add to it!! I mean, duh!! As if Steven Stevens would go round spray painting graffiti! Steven Stevens, the boy who wouldn't say boo to a goose, and if he did would most likely apologise to the goose afterwards! Brewster was obviously looking for a scapegoat. I mean, it has been a pretty bad week for the school. Quite apart from the graffiti there's been mobiles going off in classrooms left right and centre, not to mention a certain 'mysterious' infestation of rats!! Actually I feel a bit bad about that now. Perhaps if I came clean and admitted that I was behind it, they'd suspend me and not Steven? On the other hand, they'd probably suspend me *and* Steven! What would be the point of that? Maybe I should try to clear Steven's name instead? Aye, that's exactly what I'll do!

Steven • **MAY 30th**

Had 2 do it. Had 2 clean it off. Obliter8 it. Eradic8 it. Couldn't resist it. Sumthing made me do it. Had 2 B done. Now I'm suspended. Y me? Baked pot8o 4 T. Surfed Net. Bed. Got up. Wrote this. Bed again.

JUNE

Clare • JUNE 1st

Bumped into Steven Stevens in Safebury's today. We had a coffee together in the café. Honestly, you'd hardly think it was the same guy. OK, so he was still some way from becoming life and soul of the party, but he'd at least reached the point where he could look you in the eye and begin to have a conversation of sorts, without blushing and staring at his shoes! And now look at him. Straight back to square one. Right back in the old shell. And why? Because the poor bloke couldn't resist a sudden compulsion to clean up someone else's graffiti, that's why! Seb's still adamant he had nothing to do with it, even though I can't think of anyone else who'd spell 'man' with that many 'a's! But in the absence of any evidence to the contrary, I guess we're just going to have to believe him. Which begs the question, if Seb didn't do it, who did? It's almost like there's a Seb clone running around! Or worse, a whole bunch of little Seblets! Oh god, now there's a frightening thought! Never mind that just now though. Concentrate on clearing Steven's name. Concentrate on Justice For The Molton One!!

Steven • JUNE 2nd

Things 2 do:
1. Surf Net.
2. Think how nice Clare is.
3. Arrange lists in alphabetical order.

Mandy • JUNE 3rd

Clare's certainly fired up about this whole Justice For The Molton One thing. Well good for her, that's what I say! I mean, I know I take the mickey once in a while, but you can't deny her heart's in the right place. Some people moan about things but never get off their backsides to actually do anything about them. You certainly can't accuse Clare of being like that! She came into the store today to get me to sign this petition about

Steven's innocence. She's going to take it to Brewster next week apparently. Whether or not it does any good remains to be seen. But what with that, the placards, the demonstration and the occupation of the common room she's planned, Clare's certainly giving it her best shot! Saw Steven as well, by the way. I said hi, and asked him how it was going? The poor guy didn't say a thing. Just handed me this computer print-out, thanking me for my support and saying how 'gr8ful' he is!

Craig • JUNE 5th

Gordon flipping Bennet. If this is how bored and fed up I'm feeling at half term, imagine what the summer holidays are going to be like! Oh joy. Six whole weeks of Friday nights staying in while everyone else is out having a good time. Six whole weeks of my sisters getting on my nerves. Six whole weeks of watching my mum getting bigger and bigger and grosser and grosser! And six whole weeks of not <u>doing it</u> while everybody else does! Yeah, in other words, six more weeks of being me. Can't wait.

Just been round to Meera's but she wasn't in. I thought, fair enough, man, Meera doesn't need to account for every minute she's not with me. I don't own her. She's not like some pet or something. If she wants to go off and do her own thing, then fine. Respect due! Big up, Meera! Anyway it was cool because me and Mr K chilled together and talked music for a while. I tell you, man, it's an absolute joy to talk to someone over the age of 21 who doesn't drone on about all modern music sounding the same and how you can't hear the words and how there isn't a decent beat. Meera's dad is totally cool. He played me this wicked bhangra CD. So I played him a tape of my latest Hardcore-Speed-Garage-Bhangra mixes, which I just happened to have on me. I think he liked it. We're definitely going to collaborate on something soon. Why can't Dennis be that cool? Perhaps he would be if we were related by blood and not merely by name! Anyway, there we were, me and Mr K, doing some serious bonding, when all of a sudden Meera turns up. Yeah, with Clare! I mean, it's not as if Meera and Clare are best mates or anything, is it? But I was totally cool about it. Like I say, Meera doesn't have to report back to me. What am I? Some kind of sad control freak or something?

I really must look up my so-called boyfriend's chart again. Because he might not believe in the power of astrology but I certainly do! And without looking I'd hazard a guess and say that Mercury and Uranus must be in opposition at the moment. How else do you explain Seb's behaviour yesterday? It was totally out of order and frankly, rather pathetic. Honestly, what a nerve! Grilling me like that, just because I had the audacity to see Clare and not check it out with him beforehand! I mean, how dare I have a life outside of our relationship? Well, much more of this and there won't *be* a relationship! First there was the thing about not wanting me to meet his parents, and now this! I'm so angry, I really am! If I want to see Clare I flipping well will do! And besides, she needed to talk. And I was happy to listen. All she wanted to do was get some stuff off her chest. Have a bit of a moan about her parents bickering all the time. It must be really tough for her. OK, so my dad's a pain in the neck too. But for different reasons. At least Clare's honest about it. At least she doesn't come out with any garbage about being adopted! Not like some people!

Craig • JUNE 9th

I used to think Seb was so cool. Yeah, until Troy came along. Everything about Troy is, well, even cooler, basically. Even his name's cool. I mean, Craig's a rubbish name when you think about it, isn't it? Or even when you don't think about it. But Troy? It just, you know, oozes coolness. He's dead good-looking too. And yes, I know that looks aren't everything. I know that a lot of women think that a good sense of humour in a man is much more important than what he looks like. I know that because it says so in *Men Are From Margate, Women Are From Vauxhall*! The thing is though, Troy's really funny as well! I don't suppose it would be so bad if he was a bit thick. But of course he's not. He's dead brainy. And I bet he <u>does it</u> all the time! You can tell. In fact he probably only stops <u>doing it</u> so he can come to school! We're like whatsits, me and Troy. Polar opposites. It's just not fair. I bet he's rubbish at football though.

Clare • JUNE 9th

God, is there anything Troy isn't good at? There must be something! Mustn't there? Like maybe playing the tuba, or speaking Swedish or something? Although, having said that, his dad probably plays tuba in the Swedish Symphony Orchestra! I don't know, maybe I'm just a wee bit more shallow and vacuous than I thought I was? I certainly wouldn't normally be so easily impressed by someone doing keepy-uppies with a Coke can, before knocking it up in the air and volleying it straight into a rubbish bin! But I mean, the guy was walking down the street, talking on his mobile at the time for goodness sake! Call me a complete girlie, but that was seriously impressive!

Meera • JUNE 11th

Well we're still no nearer knowing who really did the graffiti, but at least it's officially been acknowledged that it wasn't Steven Stevens! That's brilliant! Clare's an absolute star, she really is! It's just a pity there aren't a few more people like her round here. A few more people who aren't all mouth and no combat trousers, mentioning no names! But I'm thinking of one person in particular. Let's call him Seb, for argument's sake. I mean, it was all very well protesting his innocence like that, but meanwhile poor old Steven was being accused of something he clearly didn't do. And what did Seb do about that? Absolutely zilch! No, it was all 'me me me', as usual! Anyway, Steven's had his suspension lifted, which is the main thing I suppose. Let's just hope this doesn't have any great lasting effect on him.

Steven • JUNE 11th

Sorted. Back 2 school. Feeling much better. How can I ever tell Clare how gr8ful I am? Can't, basically. Could e-mail her though. Discovered fascin8ing website. Defin8ly best yet! All about really interesting websites! Called reallyinterestingwebsites.com.

Seb • JUNE 12th

I suppose it's quite sweet really, man. And quite flattering too. I mean, just think, some little dude in the Fourth Year, you know, using me as some kind of role model! It's almost like I've discovered my very own protégé to, you know, groom in my own image. A bit like Qui-Gon Jinn training Obi-Wan Kenobi in *Star Wars*, in fact! Cool! My work has not been in vain. In years to come, when I'm no longer around, this little guy will be here, to carry on where I left off and to spread the word. Nice one! Except that by covering the caravan in graffiti like that, he not only nearly dropped me, his mentor, in it, he nearly dropped the whole school in it too! Just as well he got caught the second time, I suppose. Who knows what might have happened if he'd finished what he'd started? Apparently he'd got as far as OFSTED TOTALLY . . . when Miss Dubois came round the corner. Another five minutes and the inspectors would have arrived and that would have been it, dude! We could have kissed goodbye any chance of a decent report! I'm going to have to have a word with this kid. You know, big up him and massive respect for his independent spirit and all that, but if he does anything that stupid again I'm going to kick his backside basically! Er, metaphorically of course, man. I don't condone violence of any sort. Obviously. Nuff said.

Clare • JUNE 14th

Well, after all the various recent traumas and hassles, the actual Ofsted week seems to be going remarkably smoothly. I even heard one of the inspectors telling Dave that he thought everything would be fine. What a relief! It's almost like the last few days were some kind of dress rehearsal for the main event. Everything that could possibly go wrong did go wrong! Not that this week has been entirely hiccup-free, mind you! Well for a start there was the so-called Spokesdude For The Fourth Year and his flipping aerosol can! So I was right! There really is a wee Seb clone on the loose in the lower school! And let's face it, we need that like we need a hole in the ozone layer! I just hope and pray it's a one-off and that they're not being bred in some underground laboratory by an evil baddy guy, intent on taking over the world! And talking about breeding, that was a pretty close call with the baby rats! Aw, they're so cute! And the spitting image of their mum and dad too! OK, so it was unfortunate that Ratboy and Bratney chose to set up home in the Ofsted caravan! But at least we found out before the inspectors did! Mr Martin's dead chuffed to have them back again. And he's going to try and find homes for the babies. Don't think he'll be asking Dave somehow!

Seb • JUNE 15th

Yeah and another thing, man. This Troy dude is seriously beginning to get on my nerves! Just who does he think he is? Posing around in his stupid car, with his Vergucci shades perched on top of his head like that, thinking he's 'it'! Like he's the centre of attention or something! It's totally sad, man. And pathetic. Yeah, and immature.

Doesn't he realise that I'm 'it'? Doesn't he know that actually I'm the centre of attention round here? Doesn't he know that it's seriously uncool to be seen wearing a Radiophonics T-shirt? Man, they are so last week! Even Clare seems to think this guy's the bee's knees. Why that should bother me I don't know. I mean, it's not like Clare and me have got a thing going any more. Even though I know that deep down she still wants my body big-time! You know, thinking about it, maybe, just maybe it's time to start, you know, reasserting myself? Start putting myself about a bit more again. Create a few ripples here and there. We're not exactly talking Rebirth Of The Spokesdude here. Just a slight increase of profile, that's all. I mean, there's no point being anarchic for the sake of being anarchic, is there? That is just so five minutes ago, man, you know what I'm saying? So Fourth Year!

Mandy • JUNE 15th

Aaaaarrrrggghhh!!!!! I'm going to be on 'Rearranging Rooms' after all!! I can't believe it! Me, on the telly!! At last!! Aaaarrrgghhh!!! But it's true!! I got a letter this morning. From Crispin, the cute researcher guy. It says that the programme's trying to appeal to a younger audience, blah blah blah and that I'm exactly the sort of person to blah blah blah!! Me!! Mandy Miller from Molton flipping Sodbury!! I tell you, it's unreal! And he went on about my 'bubbly personality' and 'great look' and how I was a 'TV natural' and all that. Yeah, so not only am I going to be a celebrity, but it looks like I've pulled as well, ha ha!! Oh and get this. They don't just want to rearrange my room, they want to do the rest of the house as well! The whole place is going to be given a huge makeover!! This is going to be worth a small fortune. Mum's over the moon about it. She reckons she might even be able to give up one of her jobs now! Hmm, I wonder if it would be a bit ostentatious to have my own personal jacuzzi? Yeah, probably. But hey, what the heck?!! Me, on the telly!! Aaaaarrrrggghhh!!!!

Meera • JUNE 16th

Mandy's dead excited about being on 'Rearranging Rooms'! I'm really happy for her. She totally deserves a break! And I bet she'll be absolutely brilliant too! Honestly, she's sooo talented, that girl! So extrovert and bubbly and in-your-face! She's bound to get spotted. She'll get loads of offers to do other stuff. Well, why not? It happened to what's-her-face from that docusoap about lollipop ladies, didn't it? And thingybob from the one about the launderette? I mean, if she can become a big star and release a CD and be on the 'National Lottery', so can Mandy! I wonder if she'll still remember me when she's dead famous? 'Course she will! She's Mandy! She's my best mate!

Craig • JUNE 16th

Flipping Troy! On top of everything else he's so flipping good at, why does he have to be so flipping good at flipping French as well? And he obviously flipping well fancies Miss Dubois too. It makes me sick, the way he smirks and waggles his eyebrow and puts on this ridiculously OTT accent whenever he talks to her. I feel like saying 'You're wasting your time, mate! Miss Dubois'll never fall for that. She's much too intelligent. Much too classy for you!' But of course I never say anything. Well, he'd probably say something really clever and witty and shoot me down in flames and make me look like a right divvy. It's funny how quickly you can change your opinion about somebody, isn't it? Not so long ago I thought Troy was great and dead cool and everything. Now I just reckon he's a complete pain in the backside! But if you can't be emotionally fragile and a seething cauldron of contradictions when you're a hormonal teenager, when can you be? Oh, by the way, surprise surprise, Troy's not rubbish at football after all. I played against him the other day. He's actually really good. Well at least he was until I accidentally kicked him.

Seb • JUNE 17th

Man, what is happening with this weather? It's been precipitating it down for days, dude! I mean, it's supposed to be June for Seb's sake! Summer! You remember summer? That thing that used to happen between spring and autumn? Flowers, ice creams, trees, shades, blue skies? All that stuff? Whoa! Wait up! What am I doing? What am I saying? I'm going on about the weather, man!! That's what people with nothing else going on in their sad and sorry lives go on about! That's what Dennis and Marjorie go on about!! Before I know it I'll be banging on about the amount of repeats on the telly! Hopefully it's just a temporary blip though, dude. You know, normal service will be resumed as soon as possible and all that. On the other hand, this could be symptomatic of something with much more serious underlying implications. Namely that maybe, just maybe, I wasn't adopted at birth after all and that maybe, just maybe, Dennis and Marjorie really are my biological parents! Yeah right! As if! By the way, man, just for the record, there *are* way too many repeats on the telly. For real!!

Mandy • JUNE 17th

So it's official then. We passed Ofsted! All right, so there's a slight feel of 'could do better' here and there in the report apparently, but all in all we did pretty well. OK, well-ish. But definitely better than expected anyway. And a whole load better than if the inspection had taken place the week before! What it boils down to, I suppose, is we're a fairly average school, in a fairly average town. We were never going to rewrite the record books, now were we? I mean, come on! This is Molton Sodbury! So good they named it once! Anyway, at least we now know what that 'incentive' was. Yeah, a 'discothèque', as Brewster so quaintly put it, at which we're all cordially invited to 'get on down, strut our stuff and shake our funky thangs'! And as if that isn't exciting enough (and yes, I *am* being ironic), it's going to go on till half past ten! At night!! Golly gosh!! And there'll be sausage rolls and eggy sandwiches and lashings of ginger beer for everyone!! Hurrah!! I can hardly contain myself! No change there, then. Ha ha!!

Seb • JUNE 18th

Yo! Diary! DJ Sebsonic in the house and technically speaking, as of today, another year older and another year more crucial, basically. For real! Not that I'm particularly into birthdays or anything, man. No, to me a birthday's nothing more than a random date, a pinprick in the notice-board of time and as such, a largely meaningless and irrelevant non-event. Well, apart from the presents, obviously, man. Apart from that though, we're born, we live, we die. That's it. So deal with it, dude. Don't come running to me with a bit of synthetic cake wrapped in a paper napkin, just because it's your so-called birthday. What do you want? A medal? Frankly I've got better things to do, such as . . . well I think we'll just leave it at that for the moment. Suffice to say that before long, I fully expect to be officially restored to the position of 'it' once more, man. For real. Nuff said. Now then. About tonight. What will me and Meera do? Something totally slamming and banging no doubt. Hey look, I might not be into celebrating my own birthday, but I fully respect Meera's right to celebrate it on my behalf, you know what I'm saying? Check it!!

Meera • JUNE 19th

Awesome! Wicked! Fab! Funky! Happening! Groove-tastic! Just some of the words I *won't* be using to describe last night. Whoa! Talk about mind-bogglingly boring! But then it was Seb's birthday. It was his choice, not mine. Yeah, unfortunately though, his choice turned out to be staying in to watch the Digitally Remastered, Special Limited Edition Director's Cut of *Star Wars*, with thirteen seconds of previously unseen footage, plus an exclusive interview with the assistant producer's personal manicurist! OK, so it was a present from his parents. I understand that. But did we really have to watch it three times in a row? And as if that wasn't bad enough, when he eventually kissed me, he spent all the time looking over my shoulder, reading the flipping credits. Honestly, it was about as exciting as snogging a dead dog! Not that I know what it's like to snog a dead dog of course! But if that's the way he feels about me, perhaps it's time to call it a day? Maybe it's time to move on anyway? Maybe it's time to say *ciao*, Seb baby! Find someone who treats me half decently and hey, who knows, even finds me vaguely attractive?

Craig • JUNE 19th

Great. Yet another Friday night in. What's wrong with me? I should be out there, clubbing it and <u>doing it</u> like everybody else, not stuck at home with my parents, watching TV and eating custard creams! They're so gross! Not custard creams. My parents! I mean, do they really have to hold hands and kiss and coo at each other every time some stupid baby comes on the telly? I had to leave the room eventually. I couldn't take any more. Actually I was well hacked off, because 'Ready Steady Garden' was just about to start and I really like that. Anyway I decided to phone Steven up to see if he wanted to go to the pictures tomorrow. But he can't. And why can't he? He's seeing Mandy, that's why!! I mean, that's all I need to hear, isn't it? Even Steven has a life! I'm so depressed. Everything in my life is completely rubbish. I wonder how old you have to be before you can legally emigrate? Just a thought.

Steven • JUNE 20th

Gr8 day 2day. Went round 2 Mandy's 2 help clean up ready 4 'Rearranging Rooms'. U should C all the stuff she's got! Gets 20% discount from Safebury's! My kind of job! Mandy's mum really nice. Kept apologising about Mandy not turning up 2 help. Told her I didn't mind. Told her cleaning isn't exactly a chore 2 me. She asked when I could move in. Think she was joking. Pizza 4 T. Watched 'Can't Garden Won't Garden'. Bed.

Clare • JUNE 22nd

Meera's been a real pal just lately. A real, well, comfort basically, listening while I've droned on and on about my folks and their constant bickering. And OK, so I'm normally pretty sceptical about all that astrological guff she comes out with, but I have to say, some of it's been pretty spot on! One thing she didn't predict though, was yours truly being chatted up by the Incredible Hunk himself, Troy! But it's true! We were alone in the common room today and he suddenly asked me what I was doing tonight?! I couldn't believe it! I guess I'd always assumed he didn't find me particularly attractive and had me pigeonholed as some kind of worthy swot. Aye, I know, I shouldn't be so hard on myself, but self-esteem has never been one of my strong points. Anyway it seems that I was wrong. The thing is, he caught me on the hop. I was a bit gobsmacked, to be honest. I burbled something about having a driving lesson tonight and that was that. Someone else came in. The moment passed. Troy told me he really likes my car. I must admit it's looking pretty good right now. Possibly because it's so clean. Aye, Steven certainly did a great job. Again.

Seb • JUNE 22nd

Bummer. The Rebirth Of The Spokesdude isn't going quite as smoothly as I'd planned, man. Don't get me wrong. It's still going to happen. That is for real, dude! No doubt! Troy won't know what's hit him basically. Never mind ancient history, man. The guy's going to be like, instant history! The thing is, right, I've been like a dormant daffodil bulb, lying low, buried beneath the frozen soil all through the dark winter months. You know, biding my time, waiting for the right moment before eventually bursting out, more brilliant and dazzling than ever? It's just that, well, I won't be bursting out just yet, that's all. There have been a couple of minor hiccups and unforeseeable glitches. Or to continue the rather clever gardening analogy, there's been a touch of late frost, dude. Yeah well, I'd totally forgotten that I'd promised to help Dennis regrout the bathroom, hadn't I? And on top of that, Steven and Craig are coming round at the weekend to watch the Special Edition *Star Wars* again. But it's merely delaying the inevitable, man. It's all over bar the grouting! Big up myself, basically!!

Mandy • JUNE 22nd

Is there a world record for having something you've only just been given back confiscated again? If there is, I think me and Meera might have just broken it! Honestly, what a cheek though! Taking our mobiles off us again like that! What was I supposed to do? Wait until break? Yeah right! I had to phone her up! I was dead excited! I mean, come on, it's not every day you get propositioned by the school's resident sex god, is it? And anyway, how was I supposed to know Meera was standing at the front of the class, reading out her French essay at the time? What am I? Psychic or something? Phwoar! Troy, eh? Mr Top Totty himself, personally requesting a meeting with me behind the bike sheds! Meeting? First time I've heard it called that! Ha ha!!

Meera • JUNE 22nd

Ohmygodohmygod! So Troy's got the hots for Mandy, has he?! If ever a juicy morsel of Grade A goss was worth losing your mobile over, that was it!! I think it's dead exciting actually! But then I am speaking from the perspective of someone currently stuck in a meandering, stop-start, not really going anywhere kind of relationship with a guy whose idea of a good night out is staying in! Virtually anything seems exciting to me right now. Watching hair grow seems exciting to me right now! Bit of a disaster finding out in the middle of French though. I tried telling Miss Dubois it was a wrong number, but she didn't believe me. Fair enough, I suppose. I'd already been talking to Mandy for ten minutes! Lucky cow. I wish someone would ask me to meet them behind the bike sheds! The way I'm feeling right now, I might just say yes!

Mandy • JUNE 23rd

Well whaddya know? Turned out it *was* a meeting after all! Yeah, a meeting of tongues!! *Mama mia*, can that boy snog or what? OK, so there's snogging and there's snogging. But that was snogging, baby!! It was like going fifteen rounds with an industrial vacuum cleaner!

Not only were my tonsils in severe danger of being sucked out, so were most of my internal organs too! It's like, every kiss I've ever had (and let's not be coy, there've been a few!) has been nothing more than a rehearsal for this one. And snogging aside, the way he fixes you with those big blue eyes of his! He really does make you feel like you're the one! Like you're totally special! Like he'll never look at another girl ever again! I tell you, he's a total dish. Almost too good to be true in fact. I wonder if he knows how to cook and how to work a washing machine? In a way, I almost hope he doesn't. Yeah well, if he did he would be too good to be true! And nothing's perfect, is it? At least not in real life it's not. Anyway, we've scheduled another 'meeting'. With any luck we'll begin by going over the minutes of the previous one! Woooof!!

Meera • JUNE 23rd

Is it really too much to expect your boyfriend to occasionally say 'Yes, I'd love to see you tonight' when you phone him up on the spur of the moment? Or am I just being hopelessly romantic? And what's he doing that's so 'well hard and crucial' anyway? OK, so I always knew that any relationship with Seb would be a bumpy ride. I thought I'd be able to put up with it. But face facts. There's bumpy and there's bumpy, and right now we're talking practically off-road!! I think this really could be make or, quite literally, break time! What do I do? Trust my own instincts? Trust Kosmic Kate's instincts? Trust Mandy's instincts? In a funny kind of way, it's Mandy who's brought this whole thing to a head. Not that I'm blaming Mandy, of course. I think it's great about her and Troy, I really do. No, it's just that seeing her so excited and buzzing like that has confirmed what I've been thinking for a while now anyway. There's no future for me and Seb. Not as a couple anyway. How can there be? There's no spark between us any more. We're like chalk and cheese. I want to go out and have a good time! And he . . . well, doesn't, basically. No, that's it as far as I'm concerned. I'm going to call him. Tell him it's over.

Seb • JUNE 23rd

Yo! Diary! Meera's taken leave of her senses! She must have done, man. There's no other explanation for it! So things have been a bit up and down between us lately. But why would she want to end it? Doesn't she realise what a privileged position she's in? Isn't she aware that she's like, the total envy of the entire female population of Molton Sodbury and quite possibly beyond? But for some strange reason she's talking about Mandy and Troy? She's talking about how we've grown stale and how we never go out? She's talking about ending it? Check it out, right? Firstly, on the Troy front, the guy's had his fifteen minutes of fame. He should be grateful I allowed him that much. Anyway, that side of things is well in hand, man. The Return Of The Sebmeister is totally imminent, you know what I'm saying? It's sorted basically, bro'! Nuff said. As for the growing stale and not going out bit? Totally unjustified, dude. Where's the evidence, Your Honour? Anyway I couldn't have gone out with her tonight. Yeah, well I was too busy helping Dennis repot his cacti, wasn't I?

Mandy • JUNE 24th

Aw, poor Meera. It's a real shame about her and Seb but, let's face it, not exactly what you'd call an earth-shattering surprise! I mean, it has been on the cards for a while now. Well, since the day they started going out with each other, basically! Doesn't make it any easier when it actually happens though, does it? It's tough. But I'm sure she'll get over it. I'm desperately trying not to say that there are plenty more fish in the sea! But there are! Fish that are, how can I put this, slightly more conventional and less strange than Seb. Nice guy, Seb, but well, you know. Hmm, I'm not exactly sounding sympathetic here, am I? This is my best friend we're talking about after all. It's just that, well, I suppose it is a bit difficult for me to get too overwrought about the situation, what with me being in the first flush of lust myself!

Meera • JUNE 25th

Ohmygodohmygodohmygod! Just when you think you're over one dilemma, along comes another!! What on earth do I do now? Spill the beans or keep my mouth shut? Screw things up for Mandy or pretend I didn't see anything? Perhaps I really didn't see anything? Perhaps I only imagined seeing Troy grabbing Miss Dubois by the cloakroom and trying to kiss her? I mean, there were all those coats in the way, weren't there? I didn't get a clear view. Maybe it *didn't* happen that way at all? Yeah, or more likely, maybe I *hope* it didn't happen that way at all! Flipping guys, eh? What are they like?

Steven • JUNE 25th

Saw Troy bl8antly try 2 kiss Miss Dubois 2day! Couldn't help it. Was coming out of toilet + there they were. Miss Dubois defin8ly not amused. Pushed Troy away. Gave him what 4. Said she'd report him if he did it again. Troy very defl8ed. 1der if I should tell Craig?

Meera • JUNE 26th

Dilemma? What dilemma? I don't have a choice any more. I've got to tell Mandy now, before he goes and snogs his way through the entire school! Or at least tries to! And anyway, what's that saying? You've got to be cruel to be kind? Mandy needs to know what a scumbag Troy really is, before it's too late! And he's obviously not quite as bright as we thought either. I mean, fancy trying it on with me like that today! Me! Mandy's best mate! Did he honestly think it wouldn't get back to her? I don't know, perhaps he doesn't care if it does get back to her? Yeah, in which case he's an even bigger scumbag! A scumbag with lousy chat-up lines, by the way. Was that really the best he can do? 'Get your coat, love. You've pulled'? Pathetic. Just pathetic.

Mandy • JUNE 26th

Meera's an absolute gem. It must have been really difficult for her to tell me. I know she wouldn't have wanted me to be upset. But I'm not that bothered, I'm really not. Yeah, sure I was flattered to know Troy was interested and everything. Now it turns out he's interested in anything with a pulse! Of course deep down I knew it would never amount to much more than a quick bout of tonsilnastics! I mean, I knew he was never going to be the big love of my life or anything. I don't know. What is it with me and guys? I just don't seem to be able to pick them, do I? First Supermarketman and now Troy! Honestly, what a pair of utter slimeballs! Not an ounce of moral fibre between them! I mean, what am I? Some kind of lowlife magnet? Some kind of human doormat for blokes to walk all over? Well, I've had enough. I'm through with men for good! Well, maybe not for good. Good's an awful long time. But a good week or so anyway! Ha ha!!

Craig • JUNE 27th

I wish I could say that I'm completely gobsmacked by the Troy/Miss Dubois thing. But I'm not. I'm not even mildly surprised, let alone completely gobsmacked!

Let's face it, the last few months of my life have been like one big soap opera, haven't they? I mean, you name it, it's happened. Imaginary girlfriends and doomed non-existent relationships, failed footballing careers, pregnant parents (well, pregnant mother anyway) and (this one goes without saying) the ongoing storyline of being the world's oldest living virgin! I mean, Gordon flipping Bennet, what else can possibly happen? Well I suppose I could discover that I've actually been a woman all along and never realised it. Mind you, even that wouldn't be particularly gobsmacking. By the way, if it turns out this really is a soap opera, can someone please arrange for me to be written out? Thanks.

Mandy • JUNE 28th

Just got a call from Crispin The Cute Researcher, wanting to know if I was free at the end of the week? I said I was free tonight, baby, and asked him what time he was going to pick me up! Yeah yeah, I know! Only two days ago I was talking about being through with men for good! But old habits die hard. It's like a reflex with me sometimes. It's like breathing. You've just got to do it! And besides, he knew I was only joking. Well, at least I think he did! Mind you, I wouldn't say no! He is seriously cute! And who knows? Third time lucky and all that? Surely there must be one decent bloke out there with my name on him! Honestly, what am I like? Anyway, filming for 'Rearranging Rooms' starts at the weekend! I suppose I'd better tidy my room up! I wonder what Steven's doing?

Meera • JUNE 28th

Dear Leo, how are you? I'm fine thanks. Well I'm not really, but you don't want to hear all about that, do you? You must get quite enough letters already, treating you like some kind of fantasy agony uncle! By the way, I'm not expecting a personal reply or anything. It's just that, well, I'm having a bit of boyfriend trouble at the moment. You see, the trouble is . . . well, the trouble is I haven't got one, basically! Well I mean, I did, but I haven't any more, if you see what I mean? Oh, I won't bore you with the details. But to cut a long story short, we'd been going through a bit of a rough patch. You know, differences of opinion, petty jealousy, completely made-up stories about parents being lost in space, that kind of thing. Eventually I had enough. So I finished it. And now I don't know whether I've done the right thing. I mean, he drives me mad sometimes. But he can be really sweet too. And well, I guess I miss him. Even my dad's upset! They were talking about doing some DJ-ing together or something? What do you think I should do? By the way, how's the new film with Cameron Paltry going? Loved the last one. I thought the way you single-handedly stopped the ship from hitting that iceberg was absolutely brilliant. Weren't you really cold though? Just wearing that vest? Better go, I suppose. Take care. Love Meera.

Seb • JUNE 28th

Look, I never said I was any good at this relationship thing, did I, man? I never claimed I was some kind of expert. Good job too really, because I'm, you know, clearly not. I just sort of busked it as I went along. Did my own thing. Never considered Meera and what she might be feeling. I can see where I went wrong now, dude. I've had some time to do some serious thinking and reflecting. I can see that I've been guilty of dissing my woman. Yeah, and not giving her the total respect and full-on Seb treatment that she deserves, you know what I'm saying? Well check this out, right? If I can just persuade Meera to, you know, think again and maybe give me one more chance, things will be well different,

124

basically. Don't know exactly how I'm going to do it yet. But I'll think of something. Yeah, something so crucial, so banging and so totally out there, it just can't fail. It *can't* fail, dude! Sounds a bit soppy I know, but I'm really missing Meera. I'm a broken man, man. I'm in bits, baby. Seb out.

Craig • JUNE 28th

Craig rhymes with The Hague
Which is in Holland
A place I'd gladly be right now.

Maybe rhymes with baby
Which is in my mother
Please make it a brother
And not another sister
That would be
As welcome as a blister.

Virgin rhymes with sturgeon
Which is what I'll be for eternity
A virgin not a sturgeon
That's a kind of fish.

Steven • JUNE 28th

Had gr8 idea while making list of websites 2nite. How about website all about lists? 4 fans of lists. 4 people who like order in their lives. Who like 2 B organised. People like me! Defin8 gap in market! Could call it list.com! Lots 2 think about. Will make list.

Meera • JUNE 29th

Ohmygodohmygodohmygod!! Just how many last chances can you give someone? What did he have to go and do that for? The great divvy!! Why couldn't he just have been really horrible and ignored me and totally avoided me? It would have made things so much easier. But now he's gone and ruined everything, hasn't he? Just when I was getting used to the idea of being on my own! Just when Galactic Graham's been telling me I should be spending more time with myself! Oh well, what does he know anyway? He's a bloke! Honestly, who would have thought that one tiny cactus left on a doorstep could say so much? Well, one tiny cactus plus a message. 'Meera Meera on the wall, you're totally like, you know, the fairest of them all. Sorry. Seb.' He's so sweet. The great divvy.

Seb • JUNE 30th

Well it looks like it's worked, man! Seems like Meera's going to give me one last chance after all. Which is, you know, great basically. I mean, she didn't have to, did she? I mean, you couldn't really blame her if she said enough's enough, dude. You couldn't really blame her if she fancied, you know, checking out pastures new down on Relationship Farm, could you? Whoa, wait up! What am I saying? 'Course you could blame her, man! 'Course she had to give me one last chance! Hey look, this is The Sebmeister we're talking about here, not some total zero like, oh I don't know, for argument's sake let's say Troy. No, Meera's just seen sense, that's all, man. Nuff said. But listen up, right? I really am going to try from now on. Going to make sure I big up Meera with the necessary amount of respect. Going to make sure I grab this chance with both hands and don't let go, basically, you know what I'm saying? For real! No doubt, dude!

Craig • JUNE 30th

And there's me thinking I had nothing to look forward to! Silly me, eh? I'd totally forgotten about the ritual humiliation of the disco! Wonder why that is? Oh yes, I remember now. Discos are always completely rubbish and leave me emotionally scarred for several weeks afterwards. Yeah, that's it. I knew there was some perfectly good reason. But I'll still go, of course. You know, thinking that it's somehow going to be different this time, even though I know full well it won't be. Thinking that a quick squirt of Snog *Pour Homme* is instantly going to turn me into some kind of irresistible babe-magnet. Yeah, right. Boy, am I a glutton for punishment, or what? Face facts. There's more chance of City winning the Champions' League than there is of me getting a snog. Let alone anything else.

JULY

Mandy • JULY 1st

Funny how Meera kept finding endless excuses to come round to my place today, wasn't it? She hardly ever comes round normally. Not when she can phone instead! Call me cynical, but I don't suppose it could have anything to do with the fact that we were filming for 'Rearranging Rooms', could it? Not that Meera would admit that of course. No, she reckons she can't stay in her own house because of all the racket her dad's making! But I've just got a sneaking suspicion she was really checking out Crispin The Cute Researcher! Oh no, I've just remembered. She's back with Seb, isn't she? So I mean, there's no way she'd even look at another bloke, is there? Yeah, right!!

Steven • JULY 2nd

Things 2 do:

1. Ask Craig 2 help market + run list.com.

2. Float list.com on stock market + become Internet millionaire.

3. Ask Clare 2 disco, marry her + live happily ever after.

Clare • JULY 5th

Well, if you'd asked me this time yesterday whether I was going to the disco tomorrow, I'd have probably laughed in your face and told you to get a life while stocks last! I must be getting old. I mean, each to their own and all that, but it's just not my idea of fun, being stuck in a dark and sweaty room with a bunch of hyperactive kids, having some First Year throwing up all over your shoes! Aye, but that was yesterday! That was before the fickle finger of fate singled me out for a wee bit of target practice as I was strolling along the road this morning! Funny, isn't it? I mean, there I was, silently cursing the fact that my mother had borrowed my car and that I was actually having to walk to school. But then, if I hadn't been walking along, my knight in shining armour would never have stopped and asked if

I wanted a lift! And we would never have got chatting. And he would never have asked me if I fancied going to the disco with him! And I would never have thought to myself, Aye, damn right I do!! Now, all of a sudden, being stuck in a dark and sweaty room with a bunch of hyperactive kids seems like an excellent idea to me! Mind you, I could live without the First Year throwing up on my shoes!

Seb • JULY 7th

Yo! Diary! Listen up, right? Natural order has been well and truly restored to the area! The pretender to the throne has been like, you know, vanquished! Any rumours of a vacancy in the 'it' department have been totally quashed, dude! Mission accomplished, basically! DJ Sebsonic was not only in The House last night, man, he practically redecorated The House and rearranged the furniture!! Er, metaphorically speaking, of course. But resistance was futile. The beats were banging, the grooves relentless. The crowd were like, putty in my hands. Yeah, and when Mr K came on and we started mashing it up together, well the place just went into complete meltdown! In a word, it was like, totally happening, dude! We rocked the joint, man! No doubt! Big up Mr K, you know what I'm saying? As for the look on Meera's face? She just stood there, motionless and wide-eyed, looking like she was about to cry. Like she was completely overcome and blown away with the total full-on awesomeness of it all! Like she couldn't believe how close she'd come to losing me! I tell you, man, it was a beautiful moment, truly beautiful! So anyway, here's a joke. Knock knock!! Like, who's there, man? Troy! Troy who? Yeah, exactly!

Meera • JULY 7th

Ohmygodohmygodohmygod!! Where do I start? How do I even begin to convey the sheer, complete and utter embarrassment of it all? I don't think I can, basically! This was public humiliation on a previously unimaginable scale! Even worse than the time I came back from the loo with my skirt tucked in my knickers! I'm burning up inside! I just want the earth to open up and swallow me whole! Still at least I know how Seb feels about his dad now! That's one thing we appear to have in common! For the first time I can begin to understand all that stuff about him thinking he was adopted! Well hey, maybe it's me who was really adopted? It might help explain last night! Ohmygodohmygod, it's all flooding back to me again!! The shades! The combats! The backwards baseball cap! The ridiculous hand gestures! Parents today, eh? No respect for their kids any more! I mean, how could he do this to me? His own flesh and blood! Well, allegedly his own flesh and blood anyway! As for Seb? What can you say? The less the better probably! Ohmygodohmygod!! I'd better phone Mandy! After I've phoned the Astro Chatline of course! What a nightmare!!

Mandy • JULY 7th

Poor Meera. She really is in a state. I actually think it's quite sweet though, her dad and Seb DJ-ing together like that. All right, it would have been embarrassing if they'd been rubbish! But they weren't. They were surprisingly OK! Well banging, in fact, as Seb would no doubt say. Honestly, what planet is that boy from? Meera's already wondering whether she's done the right thing. And they haven't even been back together a week yet! All in all it wasn't really the right time to tell her my bit of news. About my agent calling? Yeah, I know! What agent? And why was he calling after all this time? To tell me I'm up for a part in the latest Quentin Scorcese movie? Maybe a cameo appearance in 'Mates'? Wrong. But I *have* got an audition to be an extra in a biscuit commercial! Yeah, so it's obviously been well worth the wait! Actually I was quite tempted to tell him what to do with his flipping audition! After all, I'm going to be on 'Rearranging Rooms' in a few weeks' time! Yeah, no thanks to my so-called agent! Crispin says I look great on camera, by the way. Especially good on close-ups, apparently. And Crispin should know. He's been giving me plenty of close-ups, if you know what I mean! Wooof!! What am I like? Oh, and guess what? I got my jacuzzi after all! Ha ha!!

Steven • JULY 7th

Marriage with Clare on hold 4 time being. Indefin8ly maybe? Clare + Troy make gr8 couple. Un4tun8ly. Clare much 2 good 4 him. 1der if she knows about Troy + Miss Dubois? Better not say anything. Going 2 surf Net. Search 4 cures 4 broken heart.

Clare • JULY 7th

There's me thinking I'd be spending the summer organising a wee demonstration against something or other. Yeah right! The only demonstration it looks like

I'll be organising now is a demonstration of tongue-to-tongue resuscitation!! Phwoar, can that boy kiss or what? And OK, so Troy's got a bit of a reputation. I mean, I think the longest relationship he's had since he's been here is about ten minutes! But I like to think I've got a bit of a reputation too. A reputation for not tolerating any garbage. A reputation for knowing what I want and when I want it. Aye, and a reputation for being in control! Chick power! as the Feisty Girls used to say! Sure I'm up for a good time. Sure I'm up for a wee holiday romance. Why not? But Troy should know that it's me who's calling the shots, not him! If he thinks I'm going to come running like a complete girlie, every time he snaps his fingers, he's got another think coming, baby! Oops, phone's ringing! Hi, I'm back again. Have to cut this short. I'm meeting Troy outside the megabowl in a quarter of an hour! Quarter of an hour? I'll need longer than that to get my lippy on!

Craig • JULY 7th

OK, so I didn't get a snog at the disco. Obviously. But I did see this really nice girl wearing a City shirt! I wonder why I've never noticed her before? Perhaps she's new? Or perhaps she just doesn't usually wear a

City shirt! Anyway we had a dance. All right, so we didn't actually dance with each other, but we did get fairly close at one point and I swear she very nearly looked at me! Still, it's a start, isn't it? Actually, by my standards it's more than a start. By my standards it's practically a relationship! Oh, and talking about City, Dad's only gone and bought me a season ticket for next year, hasn't he? He didn't say why. He didn't need to. It's obviously meant as some kind of peace offering for the whole baby thing. Funnily enough though I don't feel too bad about it any more. I've kind of got used to the idea now. Well, that's a bit of an exaggeration. It's still completely gross but it's going to happen whether I like it or not. Anyway, this time next year I might be able to afford to buy a season ticket myself. Depending on how things go with list.com of course! You never know, this time next year I might be able to afford to buy City! Well why not? I reckon I'm due a change of fortunes.

Steven • JULY 8th

Meera just called 2 say she'd heard about list.com from Craig. Said 2 go 4 it! Said now is gr8 time 4 me 2 expand horizons, fulfil po10tial + explore new avenues! Said things R looking up 4 me. Which is gr8! But how does Meera know? And who *is* Kosmic Kate???

When Mr. 'hey, call me Dave'
Sissons suggests that 5B keep
a diary for a whole year,
reactions are decidedly mixed!
Yo! Diary! grants us exclusive
access to all areas of six very
different fifteen-year-old
minds:

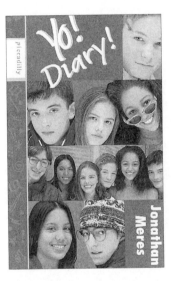

Seb – the rebel and
'Spokesdood for a
generation';
Meera – a girl obsessed
with astrology;
Steven Stevens – so good
his parents named him twice;
Clare – the local neighbourhood Eco Warrior;
Mandy – Ms Personality and Karaoke Queen, and
Craig – convinced that he's the only virgin on the entire
planet.

Jonathan Meres has written a riveting and hilarious tale of
teenagers teetering on the edge of the millennium! It's a
story of changes, drama, love, intrigue and plenty of good
old angst! And that's just in the first week!

*"Meres' strong, irreverent characterisation and sharp humour
(he was a stand-up comedian with his own radio show) make
this a book that will achieve an effortless following."*
Publishing News

Sunday 8.00 p.m.
Walking home, I said, "I don't think he's that keen on her. What sort of kiss do you think it was? Was there actual lip contact? Or was it lip to cheek, or lip to corner of mouth?"

"I think it was lip to corner of mouth, but maybe it was lip to cheek?"

"It wasn't **full-frontal snogging** though, was it?"

"No."

"I think she went for full-frontal and he converted it into lip to corner of mouth . . ."

Saturday 6.58 p.m.
Lindsay was wearing a thong! I don't understand **thongs** – what is the point of them? They just go up your bum, as far as I can tell!

Wednesday 10.30 p.m.
Mrs Next Door complained that **Angus** has been frightening their poodle again. He stalks it. I explained, "Well, he's a Scottish wildcat, that's what they do. They stalk their prey. I have tried to train him but he ate his lead."

*"This is very funny – very, very funny. I wish I had read this when I was a teenager, it really is **very funny**."* Alan Davies

THE UNEXPLAINED SERIES

The huge, eerie statues on Easter Island have always been one of the world's great mysteries. But now they have started moving and the scientific world is in uproar. What is happening? Is this some sort of supernatural event guided by alien hands?

When a scientific researcher is killed by one of the statues, Matt and his father are once again called upon to investigate a mystery that no on else is able to understand . . .

". . . *fear addicts are starting to hunt out Terrance Dicks's series The Unexplained.*" The Sunday Times

". . . *well-written and original.*" SFX magazine

Also available from Piccadilly Press, by
TERRANCE DICKS

Suddenly a man in a black uniform appeared, hurrying down the corridor towards them. He had heavy, brutal features and he had a holstered pistol at his belt. He was a sinister, frightening figure and Sarah saw that Tom was staring at him in horrified disbelief.

'Oh no!' he whispered. 'It can't be . . .'

'Can't be what?'

'SS,' muttered Tom.

The year is 2015, and the transporter has malfunctioned, reassembling Tom and Sarah in a parallel universe – one in which the Nazis have won World War II. It's a world of soldiers, guns and salutes, of work-camps and swift executions. On the run from the SS and unable to trust anyone, they must try to find a way back to their own universe . . .

"The action is satisfyingly frantic . . . (readers) will respond to Dicks' punchy style and relish the neat twist teasingly placed at the very end of the novel." Books for Keeps

Also available from Piccadilly Press, by
TERRANCE DICKS

'Sarah!' Tom shouted as he clung to the flooded rubble. 'Sarah? Where are you?'

He tried to peer through the choking mists and gain his bearings in this strange, hostile landscape.

Tom and Sarah arrive in a parallel universe, many years from now, where disaster reigns. The planet has been ruined by man's pillaging and pollution. Cities are under water, virulent plagues have killed much of the population, genetically mutated crops have destroyed agriculture and giant rats roam the countryside.

Civilisation has collapsed and the survivors battle against each other. Tom and Sarah must use all their combined courage to survive and escape home before it is too late.

If you would like more information about books available from Piccadilly Press and how to order them, please contact us at:

Piccadilly Press Ltd.
5 Castle Road
London
NW1 8PR

Tel: 020 7267 4492
Fax: 020 7267 4493